I0667301

WHITECOAT
THE CHAMPIONS OF 1940
KENNETH TAM

WHITECOAT

THE CHAMPIONS OF 1940

KENNETH TAM

ICEBERG

Published in Canada by Iceberg Publishing, Waterloo

Library and Archives Canada Cataloguing in Publication
Tam, Kenneth, 1984-
     Whitecoat : the champions of 1940 / Kenneth Tam.
ISBN 978-1-926817-50-7
     I. Title.
PS8589.A7676W45 2012   C813'.6   C2012-905207-8

Copyright © 2012 Kenneth Tam

This is a work of fiction. All characters and situations are
either the product of the author's imagination or are used
fictitiously. Any resemblance to actual persons, living or dead,
events, locales or businesses is coincidental. No part of this
book may be reproduced or transmitted in any form or by any
means, electronic or mechanical, including photocopying and
recording, or by any information storage or retrieval system
without written permission from the author, except for brief
passages quoted in a review.

First print release: October 2012
First ebook release: October 2012

Cover Photography: Olivia Witzke Photography
Cover Design: Kenneth Tam

Iceberg Publishing
171-55 Northfield Drive East
Waterloo ON Canada N2K 3T6
icebergpublishing.com

For my grandfather
Richard Joseph Barron.

And for my mother, Jacqui Tam,
who keeps teaching me how to write.

ACKNOWLEDGMENTS

Writing stories is a real privilege, and that being the case, I've been extraordinarily lucky in my work so far. Here we begin a new series that will carry on the tradition of *His Majesty's New World*, following the daughters of some of our old friends from those books, as well as a few wily survivors from 1919-1920. I am very fortunate to have the chance to share these stories, so as is my custom, I want to begin by thanking a number of people who have made this new adventure possible.

When we began work on *His Majesty's New World*, we benefitted immensely from the involvement of historical re-enactors from the Canadian Military Heritage Society. For *The Champions* our requirements were rather different, but one veteran of the CMHS has come back to help us. You'll be seeing plenty of Mark Kipper's contributions to this series, and especially to a certain Sergeant named Mike Strong. I am most grateful to him, his son Matt, his wife Anita and his daughter Christine — all of whom pitched in to help us get the history and the covers right for these books. Of course, any errors are my fault!

On the subject of covers, I must extend my sincere

thanks to everyone involved in realizing the photo fronting this book, and for images still to come: Lizz Caston, Kris Scalisi, Amy Bridger, and photographer Olivia Witzke. Bringing visual life to murky prose is rarely easy, but the contributions made by these ladies — all of them skilled artists in their specific fields — are truly exceptional.

A nod as well to the Waterloo Central Railway, and the Southern Ontario Locomotive Restoration Society, for their assistance with the images for this series. We worked with this not-for-profit group of train enthusiasts when we launched *The Reprisal*, and it's been an honor to team up with them again.

After shooting photos for *His Majesty's New World*, my very good friend Mikael Christensen is back for *The Champions*. Roaming around with re-enactors and models in historic Canadian Army uniforms somehow becomes even *more* fun when he's involved, so many thanks to him for continuing to make time for us.

Finally, and most importantly, I must thank again my partners in Iceberg Publishing: my parents. Since 2002, Jacqui and Peter have worked tirelessly to build Iceberg into company we know today. This series, and *Whitecoat* in particular, help mark our tenth anniversary... I can only imagine what the next decade of storytelling will bring. You guys are, and will ever be, the very best.

"As our society is confronted with this inequality of strength, there appear two answers. The fearful path would have us try to take power away from those who have it — from our champions. But that would be wrong, for no matter their lineage, they are now as much British citizens as you or I. No, we must not try to reduce these fortunate children to our level, but raise ourselves to theirs. We must draw from their strength, instead of trying to stifle it. To do otherwise would be proof that we are ignorant, and cowards. I say we are neither. Honourable gentlemen and ladies, the champions must be woven into the fabric of Britannia, else they snag our tapestry, and create the rip that tears us apart."

– Baron Julian Byng of Farpoint, addressing the House of Commons after the tabling of the bill that would usher in the 'Byng Policy', in 1924.

ESSENTIAL TIMELINE OF NEW WORLD HISTORY

1881 | Explorers in the Rocky Mountains on either side of the Canada-US border discover gateways that transport them to another planet. This new world teems with riches, and the United States and the British Empire partner to begin colonization.

1882 | Early new world explorers find local inhabitants, who appear outwardly to be human, but behave like feral animals. These creatures possess incredible strength and speed, and are viciously carnivorous, indiscriminately eating men, women and children. They are labeled 'savages', and their existence begins to dictate settlement of the new world.

1919 | After nearly four decades of human colonization of the new world, the Royal Newfoundland Regiment is dispatched onto the grasslands to escort Lady Emma Lee and Miss Kara Lynne in search of the source of savage strength. They discover the presence of an alien race, the Hubrin (then called 'blue men' or 'Martians'), who have genetically modified humans to become attack animals for their military. Emma Lee (more properly known as Emily) is discovered to be a daughter of these savages, who was rescued at an early age and thus developed as a civilized human being — with extraordinary physical abilities.

1920 | The Royal Newfoundland Regiment frees members of the alien Saa race (then called 'dragons') from a Hubrin prison camp and forge a partnership with these more agreeable creatures. After an incident that led to her death, Miss Kara Lynne (more properly, Caralynne) is captured, resuscitated, and genetically altered by the Hubrin, giving her the enhanced physical abilities of the savages. She is rescued when humanity and the Saa join forces to capture the Hubrin capital on the new world. During this battle, the Royal Newfoundland Regiment is almost completely wiped out, but thousands of savage children are freed at an age young enough to allow them to mature as civilized humans.

1924 | The Byng Policy establishes the protocol to be followed by the British Empire and the United States in integrating the children of the savages into human society as 'Champions'. The Lady Emily Academy for Champions is established in Newfoundland, and the Colonel Robinson Champions Institute is established in Virginia. When they reach puberty (and their abilities begin to manifest) young Champions will be sent to one of those schools for training.

1928 | The first class enters the Lady Emily Academy, made up primarily of young female Champions.

1929 | Lady Emily and her son, Robert, disappear from their quarters one evening. After months of fruitless searching, Caralynne assumes control of the Academy.

1935 | The first Champions graduate from the Lady Emily Academy, and a special military unit is formed to support their efforts to police the British Empire, under the command of the Viscount of the Grasslands, Lord James Devlin. The United States creates a similar unit.

1940...

PROLOGUE

Hearing the water in her ears always helped Alex think. She figured she was a creature of the water — not that she had any particular right to be. Her body lacked the useful control surfaces that made fish and dolphins such natural swimmers, and she'd occasionally get rude reminders that she didn't have gills... but she still felt like a sea creature.

A strange, lanky, awkward, ocean-going mammal who did some of her best pondering while she floated in calm water, letting its soft sounds lap into her ears.

Of course, she was under no illusion that she was unique in this particular preference — many people found floating in their tub, or in a swimming pool, to be a peaceful experience. Some even enjoyed doing it in a pond, or a nice lake. Alex supposed some might even have attempted it in a slow-moving river, though she'd never been inclined to give that a try.

What did make her rather unique was the fact that her favorite place to float was slightly more dramatic than all those alternatives, and to be entirely fair, more dangerous too. For most people. But the air here was better, and the company far more interesting.

As she took a deep breath of the cool, moist air that was tickling as much of her skin as was above the surface, Alex Smith looked very slightly to her left. Nothing but open sky that way — incredible blue sky looking down on an unusually placid, almost-painted ocean. There could be few more peaceful sights in either world, she imagined.

Then she tilted her head very slightly to the right and studied a great brown-green cliff towering over her. It was a sheer sheet of rock with crags, grasses and a few seagulls posted along it, all of them looking down at her with some confusion. What was a girl doing floating along a remote piece of the North Atlantic coast?

Well she was thinking. Obviously.

"Don't mind me," Alex called to her winged onlookers, though because her ears were in the water she couldn't quite hear her own voice. They mustn't have heard either, because none of them appeared to answer. Typical.

Beneath Alex the water was quite deep — she'd swum close to the cliff so she'd be out of the strong North Atlantic currents, and could lie back in peace, but the bottom was still a black mystery beneath her. There were probably fish down there, and they'd be wondering about her presence too... but those fellows had gills. Alex tended to limit her attempts at social conversation to creatures — human or otherwise — that inhaled oxygen from the air, instead of sucking it out of the water.

Not that her conversations ever got too far with the

birds. She blamed her natural awkwardness, though that didn't stop her from trying. And today might be her last chance for a while.

The weeks ahead would be very busy ones — as much as she loved to disappear for day-long swims along the coasts of Newfoundland, her upcoming responsibilities probably wouldn't allow her much time for playing in the water. Today she'd have to get her fill...

And at least the weather was cooperating.

It was one of the most beautiful Augusts Alex had seen in her twenty years, and the North Atlantic water was somewhat less frigid than she was accustomed to. The temperature didn't bother her too much either way — one of the many benefits of her special physiology — but she imagined even ordinary people might have been able to wade out into the waves on a day like this. She wouldn't have recommended any of those people try to follow one of her lengthy swims — even on calm days, the currents of the North Atlantic were powerful — but perhaps some would have been able to float.

And yet nobody would have ever thought to try.

Alex was always alone in places like this — aside from the birds, and occasional sea creatures. A porpoise had once come through, but he'd been quite rude. The fish were similarly anti-social, so mostly she kept her own counsel. But that was fine — she had enough to think about.

Taking another deep breath of fine sea air, Alex closed

her eyes and thought of her impending title — of what it would mean. It wasn't that the fate of the world would be exclusively in her hands... it was just that she'd be part of a large organization which could, on a given day, be responsible for the fate of the planet. Or, in fact, two planets. She was going to be a Champion.

No pressure.

There were thousands of Champions in the world, none older than twenty-five years. All of those who had preceded her were children of the savages, a breed of humans that had been taken to another planet by the decidedly unpleasant alien Hubrin, then genetically modified to be stronger, faster, and rather more cannibalistic.

Alex's parents had been part of an expedition to that planet — the Royal Newfoundland Regiment's mission that had discovered the Hubrin, defeated them, and made the world safe for colonization by the British Empire and the United States. They'd also freed the children of the savages — thousands of youths with these strengths, who had been saved from Hubrin hands in time to be able to grow up into civilized beings. With the passing of the Byng Policy in 1924, those talented children were destined to be Champions, and Alex was about to join their ranks.

But though she shared their strength and speed, she was different.

Unlike all other Champions she actually knew her real parents — they had raised her. She possessed Champion abilities because her mother Caralynne had been killed by the Hubrin, then brought back to life and rebuilt by their scientists to have savage strength and speed. That certainly made for an interesting story at the rare dinner parties Caralynne attended — *why yes, I was dead, and my insides were in fact put back together out of spare savage parts. Would you like to see my scar? No seriously, I'll show you my scar...*

Admittedly, part of Alex's self-proclaimed awkwardness might have come from the fact that her mother was often asked to leave fashionable society parties after she said such things (which was, of course, why she said them).

And Alex's father was no better. Caralynne had married an American drifter called Smith — a man who had mounted the rescue that sprung her from Hubrin captivity... even though he'd actually watched her die months before. Smith was wise and direct, but definitely not one for social situations. Alex hadn't even learned his first name until she was nine — he was always just 'dad' to her, and 'Smith' to everyone else.

So they were hopeless parents for teaching good social habits, and perfectly remarkable parents in just about every other way she could imagine. Smiling as she thought of them, Alex opened her eyes again.

She did not scream when she realized there was a seagull riding the breeze a few yards over her. Not at all. The technical term for her sound was a squawk, which is in fact a greeting in the seagull language.

Unfortunately, her dialect was wrong, because the seagull didn't seem to understand the noise. He just kept floating creepily above her, his stare far too intense. It was a look she'd occasionally seen before from unwanted admirers, so she knew she needed to dissuade him — but politely.

"Flattered by the attention, but... I'm here with someone. He's... a manatee. Which I will admit is unusual in these waters... he's visiting from the West Indies. He'll be right back, but he's just diving for seaweed..." she tried her excuse, but even as she was saying it, she knew her delivery wasn't convincing. Indeed, because she wasn't squawking, the gull probably didn't even understand.

The seagull proved he wasn't buying her story with his very next move: he untucked his little legs and feet, then started flapping. It took Alex a second to realize what he was planning, and by the time she did it was too late: he touched down on her stomach.

The cheeky bastard. Admittedly, his gray feathers gave him a distinguished look, but this was far too forward. Landing on her? He hadn't even offered dinner... though considering how gulls transported meals, that was definitely for the best.

"I'm a cheap date, so don't share any food, okay?"

Hearing that, he squawked. Obviously this was the gull Casanova, and as he directed a smouldering stare down his beak at her, Alex had to admit it was nice to be pursued. Despite being twenty and quite eligible, she figured she was destined for spinsterdom; all Champions were required by the Byng Policy to marry ordinary people, so their genetic enhancements could be disseminated to the wider human race.

That seemed fine for the male Champions — ordinary socialite girls positively salivated at the chance to go with the dashing men who possessed special speed and strength. For female Champions, it was rather more complicated. While Alex's father hadn't been insecure about wedding a woman physically stronger than he, the hunt for a husband was undeniably more difficult for a girl who had the ability to lift her beau over her head one-handed.

And for Alex, the problem was especially acute: she was shorter and far less womanly than most of the Lady Champions. She certainly did not conform to the pinup standards in the magazines.

So maybe she should give this gull a chance. He could fly — surely he wouldn't be insecure.

"There could be some logistical challenges, Mister Gull, but I'm open to talking about how this could work. Unless you already have kids. That's a deal-breaker."

He suddenly got quiet, and Alex realized her conditions were too stringent: of course he had kids. He was probably even married. That was it, Alex prepared to shoo off her admirer... but before she could, a dory appeared and did the job for her.

She frowned as soon as the boat drifted into view past

her feet. How had she managed to miss the noise of its approach? Champions had exceptional hearing, and even in the water she should have been able to detect the sounds of fishing.

By now Mister Gull was spooked — probably worried he was about to be found out. His abrupt liftoff left Alex floating alone, watching as the dory eased right up alongside her.

At first she thought the silence meant the small craft was empty — if there were Newfoundland fisherman aboard, there'd have been more for her to hear. There also weren't any heads visible over the dory's high sides, so perhaps some poor man's lashings had come undone, and his livelihood had just drifted out to sea.

Alex could do something about that — and since her manatee suitor was depressingly fictional, it was clear she needed to get away from this seedy piece of coast before other gulls tried their luck. Torquing her body, she let her feet fall down from the surface so that she was vertical in the water, then began to kick, just her head remaining in the air.

Sounds got a bit sharper as the water cleared from her ears, and she caught a young voice sounding a panicked cry: "We's gonna hit the rocks!"

Aha, there were some boys on board, perhaps having gone out to drop a line in the water on this lovely day, but having lost control of their little boat. The Atlantic could be very unsympathetic in such situations — barely 400 miles from this very cliff, the same ocean had claimed the *Titanic*. But today was calm enough to give the young b'ys a chance, and of course, Alex was at hand.

Without pause, she swam up to the dory, closed her hands around its side, and pulled herself far enough out of the water to see who was aboard, "Sorry to interrupt..."

The resulting screams couldn't really be mistaken for squawks — two young boys were in the boat, and both of them had that same reaction to the arrival of a sea monster in their midst.

"Holy jumpin' Moses!" was the only intelligible string of sounds Alex managed to catch amongst a healthy outburst of expletives, and it made her smile.

"Nobody's called me Moses since I shaved my beard. Mind if I come aboard?"

Even with the Moses joke, she didn't get anything resembling a coherent answer. Probably her own fault. And now both boys looked like they were going to jump over the other side of the boat, which would have been a bad idea — in her experience, most fishermen couldn't swim. Realizing her terrible humor wasn't going to diffuse the situation, Alex sank back down into the water, then kicked hard and launched herself up into the air. She landed inside the boat like an eagle touching down; her feet planted easily on one of the thwarts running across the middle of the craft, then she lowered herself to a crouch before shifting to sit.

The boys both watched, jaws hanging slack.

"My jokes always sound funnier before I say them," she apologized with a smile. "What seems to be the trouble?"

She looked towards the bow of the boat first, and there the younger boy stared at her with wide eyes. Either the beard joke had been really terrible, or her landing had been over-dramatic, because he simply continued to stare at her in shock.

But he was only nine or ten, perhaps too young to quickly recover from bad humor. That in mind, Alex looked to the stern; the older boy there had to be teenaged, and was probably the one in charge of this ill-fated expedition. But he wasn't answering either — possibly because he'd noticed that her French-made swimming costume did absolutely nothing to cover her legs.

"I'm going to have to piece this together on my own, aren't I?" Alex basically posed that question to herself, and the boy's eyes didn't budge. Great.

"You didn't tell me there was mermaids out here!"

Finally the younger one spoke from the bow, but his words were directed towards his brother. The elder boy still didn't manage to answer, so Alex looked back to the bow.

Holding up her hand in a wave, she tried once more, "Not a mermaid... though I was just pretending to date a manatee." That just earned her another confused look, so she gave up with a sigh: "I'm Alex. You?"

The boy caught on this time, "I'm Robbie. I thought mermaids had fins instead of legs!"

Alex just managed to stop her face from dropping into the palm of her hand at that assertion. It was her own fault — two attempts at jokes? She should have known better.

"She ain't a mermaid," the elder boy finally found his words, and Alex turned back to him with some relief. This time, his gaze actually met hers.

"Now we're getting somewhere — and eye contact too! Good job..." she ended with a nod meant to draw out the boy's name, and he actually took the hint.

"Sam," he said, frowning at the 'eye contact' bit.

Alex figured she best press on before he caught up: "So tell me if I'm wrong... your oars went over the side and you need to get home?"

She made that assessment quickly, based on the fact that she saw no oars.

"He dropped 'em over when we was trying to pull in a net!" Robbie declared from the bow. "Now we're going to be wrecked!"

Alex frowned at the dire forecast, "Obviously not — I'm here. But you could have been, so let this be a lesson... about oars..." It was actually even more awkward when she tried to be serious, so she stopped. "Forget it. Where's home?"

Robbie turned and pointed the way from which the boat had drifted. Alex had swum in from the opposite direction, so she supposed there had to be an outport fishing village somewhere ahead.

"Just over in the next cove," Sam added context.

That was all she needed to know: "Good. Home time."

Glad to have a good reason to escape, Alex planted her feet on the bottom of the dory and then launched herself up into the air. The boys tried to follow with their eyes, but she moved too fast — all they could see was the small splash when she re-entered her beloved water.

She knew the boys were lucky: had they drifted too much further and been caught in a coastal current, or if the weather had turned and the sea gone heavy on them, they could have truly been lost. But as she surfaced at the stern of the boat and planted her hands on its narrow transom, she knew they'd be getting a deserved reprieve — and hopefully would learn a lesson too.

"Hold on," she warned as she started kicking her legs.

Sam leaned back over the stern with wide eyes, and fortunately he planted his hands on the sides at the same time — when the dory started motoring across the water he was just able to keep from falling over.

The boat was heavy, but hardly too much for Alex to move — Champion and all — so she got up a good turn of speed and guided it towards the next cove. As she went, she looked up to the right and watched as the cliff fell away behind her. It was soon replaced by similar rock faces, but as she turned into the next cove, she saw the headlands begin to slope away from the water, with bright green grass climbing all over them.

This was a beautiful place... so much of Alex's home

island was lovely, and she figured she could spend a lifetime swimming around it, or climbing over it, without managing to discover all its secrets.

The water was shoaling beneath her now, and though the wide hull of the dory eclipsed her view of the beach ahead, she was starting to hear sounds of commotion from shore. A boat that had gone out under the power of oars was coming back with a motor. That was causing a bit of a sensation.

As the rocky bottom gradually came up under Alex's feet, she switched from kicking to walking. That let her stand, and as the water grew shallower she was able to see over the boat. Sure enough, an outport lay ahead. Small houses, some on stilts to keep them level over uneven ground, were lined up along a narrow stretch of rocky beach, and the whole tiny population of the place was hurrying down to the water's edge, releasing some cries of surprise.

Then they all fell silent as they got a look at the lanky girl pushing the dory out of the water.

With a last few heaves, Alex moved the boat right up onto the beach, sliding it over the smooth pebbles before letting it settle. That done, she took a step back and planted her hands on her hips with a slightly heroic smile. The two boys hopped out without explaining what was going on; they simply joined the two-dozen gawkers who all stared at Alex, and after a moment of quiet the soon-to-be-named Lady Smith decided she should break the silence.

"Nothing to worry about," she lifted one hand casually and waved to her audience. "Robbie and Sam just needed some help getting back. I was floating by so I stopped to lend a hand."

Perhaps that sounded a little too gallant, but Alex figured this might be the right time to come across like a Champion. At first the only answer she got was more silence; apparently the visual and the words didn't align so well. Then one of the oldest men from the village managed to respond, saying exactly what every one of his fellows was thinking: "*Wha?*"

Alex wasn't sure how to answer, but before she could even think to try, one of the women of the outport came forward in a hurry, "My God child, you'll catch your death of cold! Come inside and wrap up... glory be, you're starting to shiver... we better get you wrapped up or you'll be killed..."

As the woman approached, Alex held up her hands, "No it's quite alright, I've been swimming all day..."

"Were you shipwrecked? Oh my child..." another of the men from the outport seemed properly horrified.

Alex began to shake her head just as the woman produced a blanket and tried to wrap it around her: "No... no I swam up from Jimmystown..."

She tried to slip away from the blanket, but even her Champion speed wasn't quite sufficient to escape the mothering instincts of a Newfoundland missus, "You're skinny as anything, child! We better warm you up and get some food into you before you starve to death." The woman closed the blanket around Alex and then tried to start guiding her up the beach... only to find the girl wasn't so easy to budge as her slim form suggested. "Wha... come on, love..."

Alex shook her head, "No, you don't understand. I'm a Champion. You know, children of the savages of the new world... genetically changed by the Hubrin blue men so that I'm stronger and faster... from Lady Emily's Academy... you do know what I'm talking about?"

As her explanation drew blank looks from the people of the outport, Alex began to wonder exactly how far she'd actually swum that day. Probably a good idea to turn back before she was never heard from again.

"I'm very sorry, but I must leave you all. I'll try to visit again some day — lovely place you have here..." she deftly slipped the woman's grip, and her blanket, and was backing into the sea before anyone quite realized she'd made the move. The water was up to her waist when the onlookers fixed their gazes on her again... and then with a wave, she turned and dove into the North Atlantic.

She left stunned silence in her wake — stunned until Robbie ran to the water's edge and shouted, "Goodbye mermaid!"

That was about as logical an explanation for what he'd seen as he could figure, because he'd never bothered to learn about Champions. None of the people in this outport had much experience with them, and as they watched one swim off, they just had to shake their heads.

Returning to her husband's side, the woman who'd aimed to save Alex from freezing and starvation began folding up her rejected blanket, "She's some skinny."

Her husband nodded, but observed: "She has a pretty face, though."

With that his missus glared at him, then turned away from the beach, "Looked sour to me. And you'll be cooking your own supper tonight, Mister."

Despite being halfway out of the cove, Alex did catch that exchange (again, Champion hearing). She grimaced at the word choice but decided to ignore it. After all, Casanova gull hadn't thought her sour.

Though that probably wasn't a great vote of confidence.

There really was no way that train of thought could continue without being awkward, so Alex gave up and just swam for home. Her new life as a Champion awaited, and she was sure it would be much more dignified.

Probably.

CHAPTER I

Champion Marcus Steele yawned as he read the newspaper. He was leaning back in his chair, feet up on his desk as he tried to remain interested in the latest article about international tensions mounting at the Hague. Of course the Germans were decrying their lack of importance in the world — the Atlantic-dominated global political situation left them out in the cold, no matter how much power their empire held on the European continent. It was old news and of little interest to Steele.

Now in his mid-twenties, the American had been part of the second class to come through the Robinson Institute for United States Champions, and that seniority had bought him his choice of posts. Given the boredom he was now suffering, it seemed fairly obvious he'd chosen wrong. New York was an exciting city, and he found many girls to wow with his talents... but because the NYPD was so robust, it was rare for him to be called in to help with any particular problems.

The odd riot would break out and require his attention, but none so far this year, and most of the other crimes were of no interest to him. He wanted to turn up in the middle of a tense situation and break it apart, not spend hours pacing around, interviewing civilians and pondering who might have had motive for some irrelevant felony.

When the time came to change posts, Steele figured he'd pick somewhere more remote — somewhere his talents would make him the man about town. Until then, fighting boredom was his most onerous task.

With that very labor in mind, the Champion lowered his paper and looked across the guardroom at the officer who commanded his lance, Lieutenant Henry Lawson, "Care for chess, Henry?"

Lawson was reading a novel, and he didn't even bother raising his eyes from the text before he shook his head, "No, Marcus. Just read your paper."

The young officer sounded like an unimpressed parent, and indeed, that was consistent with his responsibilities as commander of Steele's lance — the squad of infantry assigned to keep the bored Champion from getting into too much trouble, while also providing extra hands and fire support if required. Under the Byng Policy, no Champion in Britain or America could work without a lance's supervision and protection.

Being rather certain of his own abilities, Steele had never truly appreciated the presence of the eight soldiers in his orbit. However, he had managed to become friends with Lawson — they often chased the New York girls together, the Lieutenant taking the ladies the Champion didn't want.

There were plenty; every girl wanted to go with a Champion.

But while Lawson was friendly, the lance's grizzled senior soldier, Staff Sergeant Boland, was not: "If you want something to do, we could train."

"No, thank you Sergeant," Steele raised his paper again to block out the unwelcome suggestion.

Like many of the men of the United States Army, Boland didn't think too highly of the Champion to whom he was assigned — after soldiering all over Earth, and doing a turn on the new world, the Sergeant figured he shouldn't be assigned as a babysitter for a savage-born boy who spent most of his time undressing girls who should have better sense.

Silence overtook the guardroom after those curt words. Without any better diversions, Marcus Steele tried to return to a passage in his paper about the German ambassador's outrage at British moves in Africa. Fortunately, the sound of hurried footfalls in the corridor outside diverted his attention — someone was rushing through the halls of the NYPD Headquarters...

Perhaps there was a riot?

Lowering his paper again, Steele turned his chair to face the door just as it burst open to reveal a red-faced, silver-haired Irishman in uniform: "Sir, we need you to come quickly! To Penn Station!"

Steele was instantly on his feet and reaching for his navy blue peacoat, "What's the situation, officer?"

The man was huffing, but he managed to answer, "They say... an attack..."

Interesting — it had to be something serious for the NYPD to be calling for a Champion's assistance, and of course Steele wouldn't let them down.

"Staff Sergeant, rifles and ammo," Henry Lawson came to his feet instantly, and with those orders the Lieutenant made Steele's lance ready for action.

What would they find?

Pennsylvania Station was like a great coliseum, a huge white building fronted by massive columns, serving trains that came to New York or passed through on their way elsewhere. As Steele moved towards it, he wondered which sort of train was being attacked — was someone causing trouble for a passenger just arrived in New York, or intercepting a train that was destined for points beyond?

He didn't know, but he'd soon find out. An interesting afternoon, at least.

Making his way between the pillars outside the main entrance, Steele passed a dozen NYPD officers, all of them looking beleaguered as they clung to their .38 Special revolvers. Though they lacked his abilities and weren't themselves strictly military, Steele had plenty of respect for these men — the New York Police Department was capable and professional, so for them to have called for his help, something had to be seriously amiss.

Entering the station, Steele briefly appreciated the massive vaulted ceilings pierced by large glass windows; the structure had been built decades before, but it still impressed him every time he visited. The assembled coppers seemed not to notice; three dozen of them were standing in loose ranks, a Lieutenant a few steps up on the massive staircase in front of them as he called out orders. That man fell silent as Steele appeared, the soldiers of his lance coming behind him with their Thompson submachine guns and Garand rifles charged for action.

As the leading policeman fell silent, the dozens of men he'd been briefing seemed to realize someone important had joined them. A few turned to discover that their savior had arrived.

"What seems to be the problem?" Steele asked, moving between the officers and being certain to sound as confident as he was. Something had rattled these veteran lawmen — they needed to know help was at hand.

He climbed the steps and came to a stop beside the Lieutenant before any answer was provided, and then that aged copper turned away from his men and pointed up the stairs towards the massive, sprawling lobby above, "There's someone tearing up the Washington train, platform eleven. We sent a dozen men, and then another dozen..."

That sounded unusual to Steele — for so many officers to be stopped by an attacker suggested significant skill, or perhaps some sort of poison.

Looking back towards Lawson, the Champion gave an order: "Masks. I will hold my breath."

With that he brushed past the NYPD commander, and trailed by Lawson and eight soldiers including Boland, Steele climbed the stairs into Penn Station's massive steel-and-glass lobby, listening for sounds of commotion as he went.

A train was at platform eleven. Moving steadily in that direction, New York's Champion could make out screams and whimpers... as well as a woman's insistent demands. She was asking for plans... and for a man named... Rawlings. Her voice carried easily through the evacuated station, and the fact that she was speaking so clearly, and that there were sounds of shocked people around her, suggested no poison gas could have been deployed.

"Forget the masks," Steele looked back to his soldiers, and the men who'd only just dug out their inconvenient protective gear stowed it again, walking quickly all the while.

They reached the metal stairs to platform eleven together, and Steele waved for Boland to lead the way down with his Thompson. The soldiers began their cautious descent, but Steele himself didn't wait; drawing his Colt 1911, he leapt up over the guard railing beside the staircase, then dropped easily to the platform below, landing with perfect balance.

Clearing the stairs with a glare towards his impetuous charge, Boland swept into place beside Steele and they began moving towards the train. Panicked faces were immediately visible through the windows of the nearest car... passengers fearing for their lives, and clearly distraught by what had gone on.

Unease was warranted, too; the platform was carpeted with fallen police officers — the dozens of police who'd come ahead were now either dead or unconscious. Who was this attacker?

Steele's confidence was usually quite unshakable, but he was beginning to wonder. This had to be a bold and powerful adversary...

"Rawlings? Are you Rawlings?" even Lawson could hear the woman's voice as she demanded that from inside the car.

Steele held up his hand to stop his lance's advance, then gestured from side to side. Lawson nodded and waved his hands in a matching gesture, causing his men to fan out across the platform, hefting their heavy Thomspons and their powerful Garands to their shoulders.

Once they were in position, Steele turned his focus back to the train. It sounded as though the woman was going from car to car, and he assumed someone was going with her... someone quiet, since he heard only one set of boots on the deck.

It couldn't be just one woman, surely — only a Champion could do this much damage, and no Champion Steele had ever heard of would do such a thing. Service to country was paramount.

But it was the only possibility that fit, so he had to consider it. And if it *was* a Champion, he was the only one who could go aboard and stop her. He was among the most senior of his kind, so he was confident he'd be able to master any danger... but he couldn't be impetuous.

With a steadying breath he started silently forward, heading for the open door of the nearest car. The sounds of interrogation from inside didn't change as he moved — hopefully he would be undetected. When he reached the metal side of the modern train, he stopped and held his breath, listening for more clues.

It still sounded like a lone woman, looking doggedly for a man called Rawlings. She was coming towards this car too... time for him to strike.

Pausing for a last look back to Lawson, Steele nodded, then leapt aboard the train with his Colt pistol in the lead. He turned in the direction of the woman's voice, not sure what he expected to see, and found himself facing just one lady, perhaps in her forties, with dark hair and round tinted glasses over her eyes.

She was making her way down the car towards him, a cape billowing behind her as she looked in every passenger compartment she passed. It didn't seem as though she was searching methodically at this point — perhaps this was her second time through, and she was losing patience.

Whatever the case, she appeared to Steele to be a

woman in command, and under circumstances like these, he suspected that meant she was indeed responsible for the dead and injured police outside.

"Stop, ma'am. You're under arrest."

She did stop when he spoke, but not out of obedience; even through her glasses he could see the surprise that reached her eyes as she was confronted by a man with a gun.

For a moment Steele expected her to dive sideways into one of the compartments, but instead she answered him, "You must be the town Champion."

Steele nodded, the sights of his pistol remaining aligned on her chest, "Yes ma'am, and under the authority granted to me by Executive Order 5101, I am placing you under arrest on behalf of the NYPD. Please come quietly, I don't wish to hurt you."

The woman considered him almost curiously, as if she couldn't grasp what he was saying... or what he thought he could accomplish. Steele tried to read her intentions through her expression, because it was the only response he got, but it was indecipherable.

Who was she? There was something almost familiar about her...

"Well you haven't told me your name, so I won't tell you mine, young man. But I will suggest you get off this train and not return. I will find the one I'm after and that will be the end of today's unfortunate business."

Steele shook his head immediately, "You will not."

She considered him again for a moment… and then he discovered without a doubt that she was a Champion of some kind. He certainly didn't see her approach, and he wasn't ready for the powerful blow that knocked the pistol from his hand, or the strong kick that sent him flying back through the passenger car.

The resulting explosion of pain was unlike anything he'd ever felt — beyond what he thought could be inflicted on a Champion with less than a very well-aimed (or fortunate) bullet. But there was no gun… she had used her fist.

Passengers screamed and gasped as Steele crumpled to the floor of the train car, but he couldn't afford to be distracted. If she was that strong, she'd be right on him.

Reaching up to a nearby seat, Steele got a grip and pulled himself to his feet, squaring his body and clenching his fists as soon as his balance was restored. The woman simply watched him from the end of the car, and as he straightened up she slowly shook her head.

"No need to continue," her words were gentle. "There's no reason for you to intervene in this matter."

Perhaps she sounded completely reasonable, but Steele wasn't the sort to be dissuaded when doing his duty.

"You didn't seem to have had a problem stopping the officers outside."

She tilted her head but didn't glance towards the train's platform-facing windows as he mentioned her previous victims — she probably knew he was trying to distract her.

"You'll learn about collateral damage in time. But please, young man, don't push me."

The softness of her tone was at odds with the havoc she'd created, and unwilling to waste any more time listening, Steele leapt forward. No one in the car could quite follow his move with their eyes — he was a blur, and his fists were leading the way. Brutal battering rams, to break a Champion of unknown origin.

The woman stood aside as though he were moving in slow motion, and then one of her hands shot out to catch his foot as he careened past her. She launched herself from one side of the car to the other, using the speed and violence of her lunge as a catapult that sent Steele head first into the opposite wall of the car. He groaned as his skull dented the paneling, then collapsed to the floor with blood oozing from his scalp.

It was hardly a mortal wound, but he was stunned...

Stunned but not to be dissuaded.

Planting his open hands on the floor beneath him, he started to push himself upward, looking back towards the woman who was so handily defeating him. It was impossible for him to grasp: he was a man of the 1936 class, one of the most experienced Champions in the United States. He was not going to be bested by a woman of more than forty years, no matter where she'd come from.

Where *had* she come from? It didn't make sense to him: the only Champions he knew had been rescued from the

Hubrin settlements beginning in 1920. Unless someone had perfected the use of the blue men's genetic machines, there was no way a person of her age could have come by such powers. Only two humans that old were supposed to possess...

Marcus Steele froze as his muddled mind began to reach conclusions about the woman wearing the round glasses. It couldn't be her... she hadn't been seen since 1929...

"Last warning," she said to him, but he wasn't listening. He knew who his opponent was, and why she was beating him.

Perhaps he could use some of his more advanced skills — techniques that had been added to the curriculum after her time — to gain an upper hand. That wasn't a thought he dwelled on; he launched himself into immediate action, swinging a Japanese karate kick at her as quickly as he could manage.

Again he misjudged her position, and again he felt her hands close around his ankle. Before he could swear, he felt the glass of a train window shattering against his face, and then great pain as he landed face- and chest-first on the platform, shards digging into him on impact.

He let out a wheeze and tried to roll over, but found he was in greater pain than he'd ever learned to cope with. By God she was strong...

"Marcus!" Henry Lawson hurried forward to crouch beside his fallen Champion, his own Colt 1911 up and waving in the direction of the train. "Dammit, Marcus..."

"Sir!" Boland interrupted the Lieutenant's words, and looking up the officer noted the appearance of a caped woman on the platform. Her tinted glasses were down at the end of her nose, and she was looking over their rims at the armed men there to greet her — or stop her.

"You fellows should take him and leave. There's no point you dying as well," she offered, her tone once again quite reasonable.

"Take aim!" Lawson's answer was hardly so diplomatic, and as he rose and lined up his Colt on the woman's chest, he shook his head, "You are under arrest for assault on a Champion of the United States. Surrender yourself."

Some confidence laced the young officer's words — he was with eight crack riflemen, half carrying the excellent semi-automatic Garand rifles, half carrying the Thompson submachine guns. It was more firepower in one place than an entire company of American infantry would have fielded in the Hubrin War, so no matter how this woman had fared against police officers carrying .38 Special revolvers, she'd be in tough now.

Lawson paused that line of thinking as he saw the blur of the woman's hand going under her cape. He thought to himself: *better squeeze the trigger*, but when he did the .45 caliber bullet from his pistol cracked through empty air.

Lawson didn't have the chance to think anything else, because the woman's own .45 caliber round cracked his head open, and he fell dead beside his Champion.

The sound of the shot stabbed at Steele's brain, and he managed to force himself to roll over. He was too dazed to watch much, but he did see his attacker land on the roof of the train car, and then leap again. His Champion hearing could pick out the sound of her deliberate shots amongst the hurried, almost desperate thunder unleashed by Boland and the rest of the lance — they were firing fast, trying to tag her.

But if Steele was right, this woman had been shot once before, and would have no desire to experience the same again.

As the seconds ticked past, it seemed less likely that she would have to. Her methodical firing brought down every single soldier save for one, and that man — probably Boland himself by the sound of his labored breathing — was swapping magazines on his Thompson.

He wouldn't stand a chance, except that the woman was reloading her Colt as well. If only Steele could slow her down...

Pushing thoughts of pain out of his mind, the Champion of New York forced himself to sit up and look to his left. There she stood, calmly letting one magazine slip from her pistol and drawing another from her belt.

Marcus Steele threw himself into the air, angling in her direction. The attack must have surprised her because she was forced to lean back off balance, and let the loaded magazine drop from her hand as she reached out to block his fists.

Landing on his feet, Steele managed to swing a punch at the woman's face, but she leaned to the side and then used her Colt as a club against his temple. He failed to block the strike, and the impact was like the blow from a sledgehammer. Consciousness was knocked out of him and he keeled forward, falling on her and forcing another step back.

This was the delay Boland needed; slamming a fresh magazine home, he released the open bolt of his Thompson and drew a bead on the woman.

"You will stop!" the old soldier roared at her, and she looked from him to the unconscious form of Steele and back.

Then she shook her head.

She expected that to draw brash commands from the Sergeant... a delay so she could fish out another loaded magazine while her hands were obscured behind the New York Champion's unconscious body.

Instead, the American Sergeant squeezed off a burst.

It was the most ridiculous thing she'd ever seen — typical American soldiering, by her modest estimation. The .45 caliber rounds were wide of her, but caught the side of Steele's shoulder. The force knocked him off her... and as he fell the center of his back was presented to the Sergeant's weapon. At least two more rounds punched right through the Champion of New York before the stupid old soldier processed his mistake.

Or part of his mistake.

As his jaw fell open in horror at the realization of what he'd done, Boland lost sight of the woman for just a moment — long enough for her to cross the distance that separated them. She yanked the hot Thompson from his hand and then pressed the scalding barrel to his face, drawing a savage scream. She then threw the heavy gun aside, and as he tried to stagger backward, she closed her hand around his throat.

"You killed one of *us*," she said coolly, then as his eyes bulged and he struggled, she crushed his neck as if it was made of paper.

His head assumed a sickening angle as his body dropped to the ground — joining the many others — and with a disgusted sigh the woman turned back to the train. All this blood and Rawlings didn't even seem to be aboard. Not how she'd planned it… and now the Champions might know she was out here.

But it could have been worse. She'd seen it worse many times.

For the moment she elected to leave, before the rest of the NYPD arrived with more guns than even she could outmaneuver. She'd find Rawlings another day.

CHAPTER II

Few people had Stephanie Shylock right.

At first glance, the young American was easily dismissed as nothing more than a heartbreaker — the sort of girl seen in magazines, but not common on the streets of any real town. She was tall, strong, and very pretty, and she possessed the ability to charm any man who happened to warrant her smile.

She might be unfairly dismissed, then, as a simple looker... and occasionally that underestimation served her needs quite well.

But Stephanie was a product of the American frontier on the new world. She'd been born and raised in the Pacifica Territory, and some of her earliest memories came from the war against the Hubrin in 1920, when the Newfoundland Regiment and their allies Smith and Caralynne — the parents of her best friend Alex — had been discovering the truths of that planet. Her childhood certainly hadn't been sheltered.

More than that, Stephanie's parents and extended family were smart and worldly people: father and mother Vonn and Miranda Shylock, who owned a piece of a town called Friendship, uncle Bo Shylock who was what many people called simple, and godfather Cameron Kard, who was a slightly notorious gunfighter. Her upbringing had been predictably spirited, and she was glad that she knew how to ride, shoot and scrap — all skills she'd need if her desired career came to fruition.

The Shylocks and Kard had ridden with Alex's dad during his days as a drifter on the new world, and though Smith and Caralynne had settled in Newfoundland after 1920, the families had remained close. That was how Stephanie had ended up on the rock: she'd sought the best education her parents could afford for her, and that was at Memorial College in St. John's, a popular school with close ties to the Champions. For three years, then, Stephanie had lived with the Smiths, learning the knowledge of the old world while maintaining all the skills she'd been born into on the new one.

So there was much more to Stephanie Shylock than met the eye... and she was not above breaking the odd heart, or the odd nose, if circumstances warranted.

Today she predicted it would be a nose instead of a heart.

Lacing her fingers together in her lap, Stephanie leaned back in her chair and stared at the speaker she had come to see. The young political recruiter was awfully full of himself, and for all the wrong reasons. She was barely managing to bite her tongue as he continued trying to make his patently incorrect case...

"The racial purity of our Empire is endangered by this cavorting with savage children," he said — declared, really — angrily thrusting his hands towards the ground as if he'd gone to the Adolf Hitler school of public speaking... a theory that was only reinforced by his next words. "I think we can all agree that our German brothers, Drexler and Hitler, have proven the importance of a pure race."

Of course he was a purity fanatic. No matter how much Stephanie read, she couldn't make sense of the Workers Purity Party, or whatever the Drexler-Hitler crowd was calling itself at a given time. Somehow they were attributing the fact that Germany was incapable of exceeding the power of the British Empire to a problem with racial purity? And what purity were they lacking, exactly?

It was common knowledge to every educated person that humans were humans, full stop. The Saa dragons — enemies of the Hubrin who she'd first met on the new world when she was quite young — had long ago explained the fundamentals of genetics to humanity. That knowledge had been the basis for Sir Julian Byng's policy of Champion integration into civilized society, and his determination to ensure Lords and Ladies like Alex would not be forced into isolation. If they were kept apart from the rest of humanity, they might become bitter, or develop a sense of unnatural superiority towards the people they were meant to protect.

Surely the purity fanatics hadn't missed those briefings.

There were dozens of books on the subject of genetic equality that clearly demonstrated the Champions were no more different from ordinary people than Alsatian dogs were from Labradors.

But despite the clear facts, this recruiter continued to profess his ignorant position.

"The Byng Policy... it is a travesty of the first kind. To think that the savage children should be *encouraged* to associate with true humans... to suggest that they *mate* with humans... that is bestiality. That is an offense to our purity, and it will bring about the destruction of the Empire. All the impure Empires will fall unless we take up the cause now, and purify our species. Do not allow the savage children to penetrate our society."

The fact that he'd come to Newfoundland — home of the Lady Emily Academy — for this talk was even more irritating. Most Newfoundlanders were profoundly pro-Champion, and not just because the presence of the school and its associated infrastructure had elevated their Dominion's economy to new heights.

No, much more important to Newfoundlanders was the fact that local Champions were, by and large, agreeable people. Some of the American-trained examples who came through for visits suffered from bigger egos than their British Empire counterparts, but that was probably just a question of culture. And when it came down to it, they were fine too.

As such, the Champions had many friends; it was only

a disgruntled dozen people who were willing to come to the back room of this St. John's tavern, and listen to a speaker who was proselytizing in this backward fashion. Perhaps there would have been a bigger crowd if the recruiter had been able to make his speech on the Memorial College campus, but the administrators had thrown him off school grounds as soon as he revealed his intentions.

The only ones in the room with Stephanie, then, were the true believers... plus a few skeptics keeping watch for various reasons all their own.

"You ever met a Champion?" the tavern's owner was leaning against the frame of the room's door, and his gruff interruption drew an indignant stare from the young purist.

"I have no need to interact with those creatures," he snarled back, very much in Hitler's style.

The barman wasn't about to have a fistfight in his own establishment, but he clearly didn't agree with the sentiment he was hearing. Stephanie doubted the man had known what he was letting in when the clean-cut young fellow came asking to hold a meeting. Now, instead of engaging the purist, the old b'y simply shook his head and left the room to its dogmatic hate.

"You see! That sort of laxness is what will destroy our Empire — destroy human civilization — if we allow the savage children to pollute our blood! Like the Jews, the gypsies, the homosexuals... we must deny them access to our good, honest, British people!"

By this point Stephanie had her fill. She was sitting in the back row next to the poor young man she'd dragged along as escort, but because so few people were present, that positioning offered her no anonymity when she raised her voice: "Really? Jews and gypsies and homosexuals? You know there's *scientific proof*, that all humans are, genetically speaking, the same?"

The young man's eyes found her instantly, and as Stephanie watched she could see a vein starting to pulsate on the side of his temple. Didn't look too healthy… she wondered if his head was going to explode.

But it didn't. His rhetoric did instead: "You believe the science of dragon monsters? It is that sort of naïveté that will lead to the downfall of the human race!"

Stephanie's eyebrow shot up, and she couldn't resist a smile, "I thought you just said the *Champions* were our downfall."

"There are *many* threats to our survival!" he barked back, and that vein in his temple really started throbbing.

By now people were looking back at Stephanie, and as a few genuinely angry sets of eyes settled on her she felt a nudge from her companion.

"Trying to start a bar fight?" George Devlin whispered, but she ignored the warning.

"I'm just trying to follow your logic," she prodded the speaker again, her smile still strong. "You think that because a couple of German fanatics and their movement don't like different races of people, that's scientific proof that racial purity is essential?"

An explosion definitely looked like it was coming, and Stephanie delighted in the prospect. Unfortunately, more senseless rhetoric was the recruiter's release valve: "You see how the German Empire is eroding... how they let the Serbs menace Austria-Hungary, how even the Ottomans are threatening them now. From a place of dominance they are falling into weakness, and that is because they are not pure. One day a revolution will come to Germany, and when the pure blood seizes absolute control, and disposes of the unclean, their Empire will soar to new heights. Perhaps even challenge our Empire! If we are not pure, we will not withstand them on that day!"

It looked to Stephanie like the speaker had practiced that declaration in front of a mirror. He spoke with far too much reverence and conviction... and though it probably wasn't the wisest thing, she just couldn't let him go unchallenged: "You think the Germans are having internal problems because they're impure... not because they're trying to hold onto a land Empire by lording it over long-established countries with proud national traditions?"

"It is obvious!"

Suddenly it sounded as if the recruiter thought he'd gained the upper hand, though Stephanie had no idea where he would have gotten that notion.

"You think that they're going to be able to compete

with the British Empire? Even though we have the new world and its resources... and the relationship with the Saa... and military technology that the rest of humanity has yet to *begin* to understand?"

"Just wait and see," the recruiter smiled menacingly. "With weak women like *you* here, there is little hope for us."

And that did it.

Stephanie blinked, took a second to process the words, and then her smile got even bigger, "Wait. Say that last part again."

"Dear God," George Devlin muttered as he buried his face in the palm of his hand. There was no stopping it now.

When the recruiter didn't instantly follow her order, Stephanie repeated it: "Go ahead, say that last part again. Make sure everyone hears it, so they'll all laugh when you take it back."

That sounded awfully ominous, but the recruiter wasn't about to be humiliated in front of his handful of loyal supporters.

"Who are you, and by what right do you come into a meeting like this, only to make objections? Your disrespect is typical of—"

"Of us unpure types, I got that part."

"You have not named yourself!"

Her smile grew bigger again, because the recruiter was starting to sound flustered. No stopping now...

"I am Stephanie Shylock," she said.

That name was known to some Newfoundlanders, and as she watched a look of recognition cross the recruiter's face, she thought he must have heard of her. Unfortunately, his smug smile was tied to a different supposed revelation.

"Of course, a *Jew* girl comes to defend her kind. Obviously no Jew men have the courage to face the truth, so they send a woman!"

Some of the people in the front rows smiled at that declaration, looking disapprovingly back at Stephanie. A few of those sitting in the middle rows seemed less enthusiastic, and they were more in the right (but still wrong).

Stephanie's jaw just dropped. This was too much — she almost had to wonder whether George had found some drama student to prank her, in honor of her recent graduation from Memorial. No human with the ability to dress himself could be so ignorant...

Of course he could. And with a quick glance down to confirm that George was genuinely horrified, Stephanie felt her amusement start to give way to... less passive feelings. Her fists clenched and her face clouded, and that was unfortunately all too obvious to the recruiter.

"Simple-minded Jews can do nothing but fight!"

And that really did it. Without thinking as clearly as she should have, Stephanie started forward, pushing empty chairs aside as she advanced. It wasn't that she planned to punch out the boy... just tell him off...

Respect was something Stephanie held dear. Joking

was fine, but there were certain fundamental dignities that every person was born with, and which they could only lose through their own misdeeds. This fellow had done enough to lose some of his dignity, and while she'd never considered herself much of a bruiser, uncle Bo had taught her that sometimes fisticuffs did solve problems.

Admittedly, Bo was known to be simpler than many men, but he was honest and Stephanie admired him. She'd happily follow his advice with someone like this...

A hand closed around her forearm, and as she jerked to a stop she looked back in surprise. George Devlin smiled past her at the speaker, "Come back in five years and we'll see if you're right. For now, good luck getting out of town without at least one beating."

George was no more impressed by the speaker's words, but he lacked some of Stephanie's headstrong habits. Diplomacy was his style, though for work he did carry a .38 revolver, and he was quite capable of sorting out trouble if it found him. That sort of response wasn't necessary just now; he dragged Stephanie towards the door, ignoring the laughter of the racists as well as her angry protests.

As they emerged into the wider pub he looked across the bar at the owner, "They'll probably want to go out the back door."

"Whichever way they go, it's gonna hurt," the barman replied. He'd probably put out word about who was talking, and there were enough b'ys in town who didn't appreciate the sentiment. A dustup would be inevitable.

"See, we can stay," Stephanie protested, but George ignored her words, dragging her all the way out the pub's front door and onto the St. John's street with which he shared his first name.

The mid-afternoon skies over George Street were blue and surprisingly cloudless, so as he turned Stephanie, grasped her shoulders and gave her a shake, her expression was perfectly lit. Her frown bore a delightful mix of anger, earnestness, compassion, and even a hint of confusion. He thoroughly enjoyed watching the way thoughts played on her face… but then, he enjoyed watching everything about her. Stephanie was a lovely American girl, and he was entirely smitten.

The problem, he knew, was that he'd been smitten with her since she'd arrived in Newfoundland for school, three years prior. In all that time she'd taken no interest in any man — it seemed her upbringing on the new world hadn't included much emphasis on romance — and young George was turning more into a chaperone than a potential husband. He had no idea whether that would ever change.

"George, come on, he did need a bit of an adjustment," Stephanie protested, and then a smile started creeping back onto her face.

Young Devlin had gotten good at resisting her protests, so he shook his head, "What would my father say? You're petitioning for a commission… how can he make you an officer if you're out starting bar fights? Hm?"

Stephanie switched mental gears at those words, and her smile grew: "You talk to your dad about my commission?"

George let go of her shoulders and groaned, "You're going to keep leading me on until you get a uniform, aren't you?"

As he spoke he shook his head and looked skyward, so he didn't see Stephanie move, only felt her hand cup his cheek and guide his chin back down so he could look at her, "Oh George... once I get that uniform, I'll keep leading you on. Promise."

It was almost — almost — too much to hope for. Defeated again by the beautiful American, George Devlin let out a sigh and nodded up the street, "So, does Father Conroy know you're Jewish?"

As they linked arms, Stephanie laughed, "I know, right? It's the name 'Shylock'... the Jewish moneylender in *Merchant of Venice*. You know, Shakespeare?"

George frowned, "I prefer Greek tragedies... which is probably why I like you. But Shylock sounds like an English name."

"It is," she agreed. "I doubt Shakespeare ever met a Jew in his life. But his Shylock was a manipulative cheat."

"So, more than a passing resemblance to you," George didn't miss that chance, and as Stephanie elbowed him with a smile, they left George Street and the racist meeting behind.

CHAPTER III

The Lady Emily Academy for Champions was built just outside St. John's, the capital city of the Dominion of Newfoundland, and in many respects the campus was a small town unto itself. It held dormitories, classroom buildings, training fields, firing ranges, arsenals, recreational halls... everything a young Champion-in-training could want was within reach.

Also attached to the campus was the home base for the army of the Dominion, Fort Waller. Named for the man who had led the Royal Newfoundland Regiment onto the grasslands of the new world, discovered both the Hubrin and the Saa, and died in the final battle in 1920, the base included residences for visiting Saa dragons, testing grounds, regimental barracks, training grounds and armories. It was also dominated by an imposing Headquarters that had been constructed in 1924 — a building intended to appear as grand as possible... which meant it had more rooms and open space than anyone knew what to do with.

Finally, and importantly, the whole Fort-Academy complex stood just a mile and a half from Torbay Airport, where the Royal Air Force operated its Newfoundland squadron, and from which two Saa-built skycruisers carried Champions and their lances across the world at speeds that would have been inconceivable a few decades prior.

Given the magnitude of this complex — the Academy, the Fort and the airport — and its importance to the Empire, it undoubtedly deserved a distinguished and jingoistic name. But since it was in Newfoundland, the locals had leaned towards calling it something more manageable: it was known as Jimmystown.

The man who'd fought longest against that silly name was the Viscount of the Grasslands, Lord James Devlin, because it was obviously named after him. The most senior survivor of Waller's mission to the new world in 1919 (largely because he hadn't been part of the charge in 1920), Jimmy now stood in his office on the top floor of the impossibly spacious Headquarters, his arms folded as he watched pictures flashing up on the massive Saa-built screen mounted to his wall.

"They killed a Champion," he muttered to himself, his frown deep.

Jimmy was over forty now, and twenty years of being a peer and in charge of the Newfoundland military had seasoned him considerably — not that he'd been particularly naïve after his time campaigning in Afghanistan, and his new world experiences in 1919 and 1920.

His words now were a statement of the obvious, but also carried weight... because nobody was supposed to be able to kill a Champion. Of course the savage-born heroes were human, and as susceptible to bullets as the next man or woman, but they were fast, strong, highly trained, and escorted by crack troops.

So how exactly had this Marcus Steele character been dispatched?

"The witnesses are saying it was just one woman who did it," that observation came from beside Jimmy, and as he sighed, the Lord looked to his old friend and colleague.

"Just one woman?"

"Just one. In her forties. Strong and fast as a Champion," Lady Caralynne Smith confirmed, folding her arms as she sat herself on the edge of Jimmy's desk.

Caralynne was a legend to many — once the chaperone of Lady Emily, she had been captured and genetically rebuilt by the Hubrin blue men. Now she possessed all the powers of a Champion, and had passed those powers to her daughter Alex. She had been running the Academy since Emily's disappearance eleven years prior, and she was an indispensable ally for the Viscount.

Jimmy looked back to the visuals on the screen as an NYPD cameraman swept the platform with his lens, showing all the fallen coppers and soldiers... then stopping on the late Champion Steele. One woman with savage strength and speed... in her forties... there were only two humans in existence who could be suspects, and one was in the room with him.

"I was with Smith the whole time. Promise," Caralynne volunteered her alibi dryly. "So you know what that means."

Jimmy did know. Lady Emily, who in 1929 had disappeared with her son — late-Colonel Tom Waller's son — was the only suspect. But what sort of madness could have possessed her to do something like this?

She had been the first civilized child of savages in the history of either world, having been rescued from those genetically-modified creatures as a young girl and raised in Canadian and British society. When her strengths had become apparent she'd been made a Lady, and with her surrogate sister Caralynne she was eventually sent back to the new world to seek out the reasons for her powers. That had been where Jimmy had first met both Emily and Caralynne, and where he and the Royal Newfoundland Regiment had discovered the alien Hubrin, as well as their enemies the Saa. Those discoveries had led to brutal battles as British Imperial troops sought to secure a place for humanity in the midst of an interstellar war.

Returning from those battles pregnant and without her lover, Emily had hardly been stable. Her entire life had been emotionally trying, and she had no real parents to call her own, so it had been left to people like Caralynne and Jimmy to help her find her way through motherhood. She'd been given some purpose with the establishment of an Academy for rescued children of the savages — children who were coming to civilization the same way she had. That had seemed to help her find her feet...

Until she disappeared without a trace that night in 1929, taking young Robert with her.

Since then there had been intermittent sightings, but no more than that. Was killing the Champion of New York her reintroduction to the world?

"If it is her... and we don't know that it is... what's she after?" Jimmy finally stopped his expository pondering and asked his question before releasing another sigh.

Caralynne had been ready for the query, "Witnesses say she was looking for plans, and for a man called Rawlings."

Jimmy began to nod, but stopped himself as he realized he actually recognized the name.

"Sir Benjamin?"

"I'd assume so," Caralynne agreed. "He's liaising with the War Department, showing them the blueprints for Snapdragon."

Jimmy had indeed heard of this; Rawlings was one of the engineers working on new-generation airplanes for the Royal Air Force — planes that incorporated the improved understanding of metallurgy and physics provided to British scientists by their Saa allies. Snapdragon was reportedly going to be a revelation for air combat... it would render the current-generation Spitfire quite obsolete.

Of course, being in a close alliance with the United States — the only other government on Earth with access to the new world, and to Champions — the Empire was offering plans and expertise to the American armed forces.

That meant Rawlings was going to Washington… with everything one could possibly need to steal if, for instance, one's intent was to help arm those who meant to challenge British-American hegemony.

If it was Emily… then what was her aim?

"Rawlings wasn't on the train," Caralynne continued her explanation as Jimmy wandered through his own thoughts. "The War Office was clever enough to book him under an alias on an earlier one… this was just a decoy in case anyone happened to be paying attention."

"Apparently someone was," Jimmy replied. "Probably would have helped poor Mister Steele if someone had informed the NYPD."

Caralynne nodded, "I believe that feedback has already been passed along. But this did work… it flushed out a would-be thief. A powerful one."

Yes it had worked, and as Jimmy acknowledged that truth with a nod, he found himself wondering about the implications. He was, amongst many other things, the commanding officer of the British Empire's regiment of Champions. The unit bore his name — Viscount Devlin's Own Special Service Regiment (or more commonly, Lord Jimmy's Own Champions) — and it was unlike anything else the Empire had ever organized. With the threat of a rogue Champion on the loose, it was likely the only formation that could be called upon for a response.

"We'll have to deploy lances to protect everyone on the Snapdragon project," the Viscount said after a moment's thought. "Is Rawlings still in Washington?"

Caralynne nodded, "Our counterparts at the Robinson Institute have put him under triple guard. But I still wouldn't send him back to Toronto by train."

A very prudent point, and Jimmy agreed: "We'll send a cruiser for him. Meantime, we'll send teams to Toronto and London with extra guards for the research team."

That seemed to make the most sense, and with the decisions made, Jimmy found his attention returning to the moving pictures on his screen. There was no doubt Steele's brutal killing was consistent with Emily's work against the savages in the old days...

But he wasn't going to dwell on the possible implications of that — at least not for now.

"I'll start sorting out who gets dispatched where. If you've got ideas for good pairings, I'd appreciate it," the Viscount forced his focus away from the screen, then rounded his desk and pulled out his chair.

Coming back to her feet, Caralynne turned to face him, "I'll look at who's available. We don't have that many reserve lances, so we'll have to put stronger Champions with weaker ones."

"Fair enough," Jimmy concurred as he sat. "I suppose we should have planned for his... just never figured we'd have to send our own out against... well."

He obviously didn't need to finish the sentence — no one had expected that Champions would be expected to duel Champions... at least not any time soon. There was always the fear that seeing themselves as superior, the savage-born heroes would attempt to seize control of the Empire, but that was why Sir Julian Byng, while Governor General of Canada, had forced the ratification of the policy that bore his name.

Champions were expected to spend their lives alongside ordinary humans, and even to marry ordinary persons, so that they never felt apart from the broader population. The racialists... or racists, as they were called these days... complained to high heaven about that supposed pollution of the human bloodline, but Jimmy figured Sir Julian had been right.

Better that the savage-born Champions have close ties to those who didn't share their gifts — better they realize that, in the end, they were humans just like everyone else. If they lost that perspective, who knew what they'd become...

What Lady Emily had perhaps become during her absence.

"There's something else, Jimmy," Caralynne's abrupt interruption disrupted the Viscount's musing, and he looked up at her again. The expression on her face had changed slightly; she clearly hadn't forgotten the serious situation they faced, but something else was on her mind.

Jimmy figured it out immediately: "Ah yes, I have the

letters creating Alex as a Lady. Still think the letters should be redundant, since you're one... but yes, as soon as I finish the paperwork she can join the Regiment. If you still want her to."

Caralynne didn't particularly want to think of her daughter being involved in the missions they might soon embark upon — joining the Champions at just the moment when their work seemed to be growing more dangerous — but it wasn't her choice. As her husband had insisted, it was for Alex to choose her life's path, and she wasn't inclined to teach at the Academy.

"You know it's her decision," Caralynne voiced that sentiment simply, and Jimmy sat back in his chair and somehow managed to smile.

"Strong-headed as her mother?"

"As wise as her father," Caralynne countered, smiling a little. She had been married for twenty years, and much the way Jimmy and his wife remained incredibly close, she and Smith had never wavered. He was the man who'd come back for her, after all — who'd risked everything to find her, even when he'd known she was dead.

"I'll make sure she gets posted somewhere appropriate to her experience level, just to start with," Jimmy offered his assurance, and Caralynne nodded in appreciation.

"Thanks..." her words trailed off for a moment, then she folded her arms again as she thought of the other girl living under her roof. "What about Stephanie?"

Lord Jimmy let his head fall back against the leather headrest of his chair, "You too? George won't quit asking."

"She wants to be an officer. And she's as qualified as any other youngster you take on," Caralynne made her case firmly, and Jimmy released another sigh.

Stephanie Shylock was an able rider, a skilled shooter, and was reputed even to have the canniness to beat an attacker with her fists. She was more intelligent than two thirds of the senior officers in the regiment, and no less smart that the rest. She was, in short, a prime candidate to be put in charge of some of his men.

She just happened to be a woman.

Jimmy was never the sort to pre-judge people for their sex. Aside from his profound respect for his wife, Annie, he'd seen Emily and Caralynne both defy the expectations of womanhood on the new world. Indeed, even the Saa liaison to his regiment — his old friend Sass — was a female dragon who also happened to be a starship engineer, a mother, and the size of a whale.

But enlightened though Jimmy was, he knew that some places his officers were expected to go wouldn't be so forward-thinking. He was rather protective of Stephanie, even though she wasn't his daughter (at least not yet, since George seemed to be having no luck) so the thought of her leading men into some backward corner of the globe…

"Jimmy," Caralynne snapped her fingers a couple of times, summoning him back to reality. "You're not going to disappoint her, right?"

Looking up at the insistent eyes of his old friend, he sighed. Stephanie did have the approval of her parents — he'd received two letters from Miranda and Vonn Shylock — as well as the endorsements of numerous luminaries from Memorial College. It was in his power to commission anyone he wished as an officer in his Special Service Regiment... he'd even made Sass a Colonel, and she wasn't human.

So he supposed there was no way out.

"She can be the officer for your daughter's lance," he conceded grudgingly, sounding only a tiny bit defeated. "God help whatever Sergeant we assign to them."

Caralynne began to smile at that, but found herself immediately beginning to wonder about the identity of that NCO. Who exactly could they put with two headstrong girls, and expect to keep them in line... even keep up with them?

They'd soon have to decide; the newest Champion and her lance were about to join Lord Jimmy's Own Champions.

CHAPTER IV

For many years of his life, Smith had never figured on settling down, having a house or a family. Now he had both, and sitting on a rock not far from his home, overlooking the narrow rocky beach that his land backed onto, he marveled at how things had evolved.

It wasn't that Smith was a completely different man than he'd been when he'd ridden his horse on the new world trails, Colt New Service revolver and Winchester '92 always close at hand. Many parts of himself he figured were the same. But back in 1920, on the eve of going out to look for Caralynne based on some uncertain information he'd secured from a Hubrin officer, Smith had made a decision to settle down. It had actually been Stephanie herself — just three years old at the time — who'd helped him decide. A picture she'd drawn for him, of a family he'd hoped one day to have, now hung on the wall in his study.

Things had worked out right since then. Only his horse — his trusty Appaloosa mare — was missing now. She'd disappeared years prior, and Smith figured she'd just known it was her time to go. He missed her — had yet to replace her — but people mattered much more.

The former-drifter had made sure he was never again parted from Caralynne, and though they'd only been able to have one daughter, Alex was his pride and joy. Together with Stephanie living in their house for the past few years, Smith found his ladies helped him appreciate life in a way he couldn't have imagined a few decades before. He was settled, and soon his daughter would be the one roving the world... worlds... for her own adventures.

As far as Smith was concerned, she was already off to a fine start. From his rock perch, he was able to see the splashes coming through the calm water out by the headland, a sure sign that his daughter was on her way in from her day-long swim. When she'd been younger, both Smith and Caralynne had occasionally worried when Alex disappeared into the Atlantic. Only once had that been warranted — a gale had come up and she'd been pushed out to sea, where she'd surprised a schooner Captain by coming aboard with his load of cod. She'd only been fourteen when that happened, and it had taken two weeks for her to stop smelling of fish. Ever since then she'd learned how to swim within her limits, so when she went off for a day, her parents just trusted she'd be back.

And she always was.

Now she was cruising towards the family beach, and redirecting his gaze downward, Smith saw that Stephanie was down there waiting. The girls were inseparable — much as Caralynne and Emily had once been — and Smith was pleased by how little he ever saw them quarrel. Some people told him and Caralynne that the girls were too good to be true... that it was impossible for daughters to be so level-headed, or young girls to be so good to each other. Smith didn't know what that was supposed to mean, he just knew what was: his girl, and Vonn and Miranda's girl, were a real team. And he was glad.

Once they were out having their adventures in the worlds, it was just going to be important to make certain they had the right Sergeant with them. That was the subject that had been preoccupying Smith since he'd received a telephone call from Caralynne — she used the special line that connected the Headquarters to their modest home (in case she was ever needed for an emergency) to let her husband know the news about Stephanie and Alex.

It was all to be official beginning the very next day — coat to be chosen, uniform fitted. So they had to decide on a Sergeant, and because of the respect Smith commanded, he was going to have a say.

But who? The former-drifter wasn't so well acquainted with the soldiers of the Special Service Regiment, or the Newfoundland Regiment, as he'd once been... but he still knew a few of the best. Recognizing this decision was ahead, he'd spent weeks trying to decide between them.

Colour Sergeant Cooper was a veteran of Waller's last charge on the grasslands... a man who was grim and steady, and would make certain the girls always had a voice of sense around to keep them out of trouble.

There was also Sergeant Strong, another veteran who had a reputation with women but was a good soldier on all fronts except discipline. He'd been demoted from Colour Sergeant for punching out the Minister of War after a disagreement about that politician's wife. He had a sense of humor and little respect for undeserved authority, but he'd be able to keep up with the girls' wit.

Last there was King, who was the least likely to do the job, since he was the Regimental Sergeant Major for the Royal Newfoundland Regiment. Still, Smith knew that man from the old days and could ask, if the fit was right.

It was a decision Smith would make after talking with Caralynne, and together they'd take their recommendation to Jimmy. Soon they'd choose... but first, the girls themselves had to be informed, and the former-drifter would wait for his wife to get home for that.

When Alex's feet touched bottom she straightened up and then stretched her arms out over her head. A full day's swim was a fine workout, and she always felt exhilarated when she finished one... until she ate a huge dinner and passed out before the sun went down.

But even that was exciting — she always dreamed nice dreams after a long swim. Perhaps it was the water, perhaps the depth of the fatigue, but either way, she was looking forward to a huge supper and a warm bed.

As she strode out of the water, stretching and sniffing the air in hopes of catching the first whiff of dinner being prepared at the house above the beach, she noticed Stephanie was sitting on a log, waiting for her.

Seeing her friend was on dry land, the American girl picked up the towel she'd brought from the house and lobbed it, "Good day?"

"I got mistaken for a mermaid," Alex smiled as she caught the towel and wrapped it around her shoulders.

"Drunk or young?"

"Young. Couple of boys adrift in a dory, but I got them home."

"I'll bet you did," Stephanie answered with a smile.

"Younger than that," Alex clarified as she crossed to her friend's chosen log and perched herself on the edge. The young Champion then discovered the dried wood was less comfortable in a swimming costume than it probably was for Stephanie wearing trousers, so she shuffled forward and lowered herself to sit on the fine rounded pebbles of the beach.

"Attractive older brothers grateful that you rescued their wayward boys?" Stephanie continued to tease, and Alex shook her head as she dried her hair. Already the salt left behind by evaporating water was starting to make her feel gritty, so a bath would be in order.

But that would mean she'd have to wait for dinner. Eating was one of her purposes for living, so she wasn't sure how she felt about that.

Ignoring the great dilemma, Alex continued with the story of her day, "No brothers, just outport people who thought I was shipwrecked, starving, and sour. Closest I came to a suitor was a seagull. He actually landed on me. But I think he was married."

"They always are," Stephanie nodded seriously. "They get you with the distinguished gray feathers, but really they're just sick of their wives squawking at them."

Alex waved her hand at her friend, "Exactly. I tried to scare him off, too — told him I was dating a manatee."

"Manatees always seem so happy," Stephanie observed most approvingly.

"I know! But it didn't even faze him," Alex continued her account with a shake of her head. "In the end, he just landed on me, squawked, and flew off. Didn't even bring me dinner."

Frowning at that, the American girl paused before replying, "Are you complaining that he didn't regurgitate fish onto you?"

"I'm just saying that it'd be nice if he made the effort."

Stephanie's eyebrow climbed at the assertion, "I realize you love food, but."

Holding up her hand, Alex shook her head, "I know, I'm complicated."

"People call themselves complicated for many reasons," Stephanie shook her head. "This one's new."

● ● ●

Smith could hear the animated tones coming from the beach below, but was too far away to make out words. Whatever was being said, it was certainly the happy repartee his girls shared, and Smith appreciated its joyful texture. Soon, though, he was diverted by new sounds coming from the woods behind him.

Because the Smith house backed right onto the sea, it was separated from the rest of Jimmystown by a stand of trees that afforded a certain amount of privacy... and which meant a silent approach was difficult, even for a woman possessing the talents of a Champion.

Well, Caralynne probably could have snuck up on most ordinary people, but Smith had spent too many years drifting on the new world. The many skills he'd learned there were the reason he still taught the advanced tracking classes at the Academy — Champions who took to his lessons were almost impossible to surprise, just like he was now.

"How are you?" Smith was an economical man when it came to words, so while the question might have sounded cool to an uninitiated outsider, it was almost flowery to Caralynne's ears.

Arriving beside her husband, she took a breath and shook her head, "They'll be official as of tomorrow. But the timing might be terrible."

Their earlier telephone conversation had done much to preview the day's news, so now Smith followed up with an important question: "Emily?"

Caralynne's eyes settled on the beach below as she shook her head, "We don't know for certain. But logically, I don't know who else could have done it."

The entire notion that Emily had come back after her disappearance, and was apparently working against the Champions in some way... it was not the sort of thought any sensible man could find appealing, and Smith reckoned he was sensible.

Still, Caralynne's concern for their daughter — the only child they could ever have — was premature, and as the former-drifter reached up and took his wife's hand with his, he said so: "They'll stay close to you, and they'll take care of each other."

He said it with certainty, because he knew his girls. Alex was sometimes anxious because she felt awkward, and her body wasn't like those of the pinup girls from magazines. Stephanie could be too fast to create trouble over something she believed, and quietly feared being underestimated for looking like she did come from one of those magazines. But they were young — Smith figured it was normal they had some things to decide about themselves. And whatever preoccupied them when they were at ease, Smith knew both girls were sharper than he himself had ever been. And stronger too.

Worrying about them — especially Alex, because she was his blood — was right for him to do. But having lived so much of his life without a path, and without someone close by to rely on, Smith reckoned these two had the odds stacked in their favor.

And soon a third would join their team, making them stronger... if he was the right man.

"We need to choose a Sergeant. Jimmy says it's up to us," Caralynne might as well have been hearing Smith's thoughts when she said that, and the drifter nodded.

Listening to the laughter below, he answered his wife: "We should probably give them the good news first."

Caralynne was only half as eager for that moment as she'd expected to be... but Smith was right.

"You or me?" she asked.

Smith didn't mind either way, so he simply tilted his head, "Either."

It was a typical relaxed answer from the American, so Caralynne took a breath and then raised her voice slightly: "Alex, come up here. And bring your Lieutenant with you. Big day tomorrow."

There was silence for a second after those words, and then a couple of squawks of glee from the beach below. Knowing what was next, Smith rose to his feet — he was a little stiff, his body having weathered enough in its fifty years to slow him down, but he braced himself properly so that when Alex appeared from thin air and nearly tackled him with her waterlogged hug, he didn't fall over.

"Congratulations, Lady," he said to his daughter as she

embraced him, and she closed her eyes as she squeezed him as tight as she dared (without crushing him).

"Love you dad."

Smith was not a good man when it came to affection and words, but he'd learned the best thing to say to his daughter in such moments was the plain truth, "Love you. Proud of you."

Other hugs had to be traded, and the news about the New York attack had to temper moods some, but Smith was only partially aware of those conversations as they happened. A Sergeant needed to be chosen, and he was determined it be the correct one.

A man called...

CHAPTER V

"Strong!"

The Caribou Hut was a popular club for servicemen in St. John's — a home away from home for those in uniform looking for a place to stay in town. Run by a civilian committee of local notables, the Hut was in fact a five-storey building, complete with amenities like a pool, a card room, and a kitchen that served the best in Newfoundland home cooking to men who were far too accustomed to what their army, navy or air force might normally feed them.

It was also a dry club — drinking could be done all along George Street, so there was no reason to let booze be served within its walls. If a serviceman came in drunk to sleep off a long night, that was fine, but no drunken behavior would be tolerated inside.

Indeed, with the number of volunteer grandmothers who attended the Hut, to mend socks, cook and counsel, it was expected that the place was to be entirely virtuous — something undeniably remarkable for a soldier's hostel. And for the most part, that expectation was respected.

Some men, however, needed reminding of the behavior standards, and as a crowd of sailors from the Royal Navy destroyer *Inglefield* poured out onto the street in front of the Hut, it was one of their bosuns who had been told to expect a lesson.

A big Irishman named McKenna, the bosun was rolling up his sleeves as he called out his opponent. His sailors joined in — they had no idea who this Strong character was, and half of them had no idea what his beef was with their shipmate, but they didn't care: a good fight was always welcome entertainment, and when a man as senior as the bosun was involved, that usually meant there had to be reason for it.

While the Brits collected on the sidewalk to the left of the club, a crowd of Newfoundlanders — soldiers mainly from the Royal Newfoundland Regiment and Jimmy's Own Champions — began to collect on the right. Among them was a big man who had once held the esteemed rank of Colour Sergeant... but who'd lost that (and the ability to gain any further promotion) when he'd been discovered to have a certain rapport with the Minister of War's wife.

No soldiers held that against him, of course — many patted him on the back, because the fat old Minister of War had wed a girl barely old enough to vote — and so they still honored him by calling him by the rank he no longer held: "Colour! Colour!"

Mike Strong was a very experienced soldier. He'd been on the new world with Tom Waller and Jimmy Devlin; he'd found the Hubrin with the b'ys, had fought at Promised

Town, Fort Martian, in the Badlands and of course had been part of Waller's last charge against the Hubrin capital. He'd been one of two men to carry George Tucker's stretcher into that city... he'd been one of the few to survive.

And those experiences — being one of sixty-eight men from more than 1,000 to survive those years — had left a mark on him. He'd never married, never tried for a family, but instead had earned a reputation for going with girls who were far too young to waste their time with him... to being a well known Lothario. People figured that was Strong's right — he was a good soldier and he could relax in whatever way suited him — but it did lead to the odd scrap now and then... and the bosun was next.

Because he'd had a go at Daphne, a girl who worked in the kitchen of the Hut, and who was well known to be one of Colour Strong's young ladies.

"Come on, Colour!" one of the b'ys from the Royal Newfoundland Regiment slapped Strong on the back as he stripped off his battle dress blouse, and then rolled up the sleeves of his shirt.

With a smile to that man, Strong winked, "I'll have this done quick, someone better have a pint ready!"

The bosun from *Inglefield* heard that boast, and he called out to his opponent, "We going to square this or are you just gonna to talk about it?"

"Come on then," Strong turned those words against the Irishman, and strode out from the crowd of b'ys who were ready to cheer him on and join in if the sailors of the Royal Navy destroyer tried to mix it up. That ship hadn't been in harbor long enough to know the dangers of starting a brawl with the Newfoundland Regiment… and to be equally fair, the Newfoundlanders didn't know better than to start something with a crowd of sailors who'd probably seen brawls in ports all over the world.

Either way, Strong didn't plan on letting this get too far out of hand.

As the bosun came towards him, the burly sailor made his final address: "You make your peace with God, Strong."

Grinning, the Sergeant clenched his fists, but kept them at his sides, "You talk like an Irishman, McKenna… but when it comes to fighting I think you should govern yourself with one question only."

The Irishman scowled at that, then rather conveniently accepted the invitation to ask for clarification: "And what question is that?"

Mike Strong swung from the hip in a way McKenna hadn't quite been ready for, and as the big Sergeant's fist connected with his sizable gut, the bosun wheezed.

Then the Sergeant grappled close to the half-winded Irishman, and growled the answer: "What would Mike Strong do?"

That, of course, was the Sergeant's very own catch-phrase — one he'd use at any possible occasion, especially when it didn't make sense. Right now the cooperation of the bosun had almost made it seem sensible, so Strong was pleased. He stepped back and wound up again, then crossed the bosun's jaw with a solid haymaker that sent him back onto his backside on the sidewalk.

"Colour! Colour!" the b'ys chanted, pleased to see one of their own triumphant over the limey sailor who'd dared to try a grope of Daphne's thigh.

Obviously pleased with himself, the big Sergeant turned back to his men and raised his hands in victory. Two punches and it was finished — one of the uncommonly easier bouts he'd been involved in, and as he grinned and basked in the glory of his victory, he did actually stop to question himself: *what would Mike Strong do (if he'd been knocked on his ass after two punches)?*

Shit.

Strong only managed to turn halfway back towards McKenna before the big Irishman hurtled into him. It was almost a rugby tackle, and the Colour barely got his arm out to keep him from going headfirst into the sidewalk.

"Ye bastard!" the bosun was roaring, and Strong flailed and tried slapping the big man on his head. It didn't really help.

The crowd of Newfoundlanders howled as their Sergeant went down, and then as the Irishman drew back enough to rear up and present his fists, they started heckling him — in turn earning themselves the jeers of the *Inglefields*. It was a proper fight after all...

Strong swung his leg around to knock McKenna off him, but the bosun was more prepared for this one, and instead wound up and punched the Sergeant across the jaw. It was a pretty good shot — not the worst the Colour had ever absorbed but respectable. His head snapped back and he was left stunned for a second.

Taking his chance, the Irishman then half-crawled up alongside the Newfoundlander, wound up, and punched straight for his nose.

But despite what people who had conversations with him might expect, Strong wasn't quite as stunned as he sometimes pretended to be. Swinging his head aside at the last second, he left the bosun's fist to hit pavement, and the man let out a prodigious yell as skin and bone lost that particular fight.

Then Strong sat up and rolled away, getting his feet under him as quick as he could. He never fought sitting down if he could help it. McKenna's hand was torn up, but the big sailor was far from beaten, so he hurried to his feet as well, then both men puffed up for another round, cheered on by the servicemen eager to see their respective warriors victorious.

Of course, they knew the fight could be cut short at any moment by the arrival of Shore Patrol — brawling was never looked upon favorably in St. John's, even when businesses weren't being damaged because of it.

"I'll show you what Mike Strong will do!" McKenna

decided to call back the question as he erupted with red-faced rage, and hearing the line, Strong grinned with delight.

"He's using my catchphrase!"

The two big men then hurled themselves at each other…

And got an abject lesson in stopping fast when a fine looking lady stepped between them.

It was undoubtedly a courageous act — the woman was too advanced in years to be a Champion — but her fine clothing combined with her air of authority stopped the bosun pat.

Mike Strong, on the other hand, stopped because he knew better than to so much as accidentally bump his own dearest and sainted mother.

Of course, Lady Anne Devlin, the Viscountess of the Grasslands was not actually Mike Strong's mother — for one thing, she was years younger than him, and her own son George wasn't even yet twenty.

But to every Newfoundlander in uniform, the wife of Lord Jimmy was indeed a sainted mother figure: Anne, formerly and still occasionally known as Annie, was the matriarch of Jimmystown. And her expression as she stepped into the middle of this particular fight was not terribly sympathetic.

"Bosun!"

While Anne needed to say nothing to halt a fight, Captain Percy Todd of *Inglefield* was more inclined to verbally express his anger at the situation. It was bad timing that both he and the Viscountess had been leaving a special dinner at the Ivory Wharf, just down the street, and had come to see what the commotion was about.

"Sir!" the bosun was immediately at attention, as were the men from the destroyer.

Todd was an experienced officer, and as he rounded his burly sailor he wore an expression that typified British discipline, "I suppose there's a good reason for this, bosun?"

Seeing the heat that was about to come, Mike Strong again recited his question to himself, and figured out his answer: "Excuse me, Captain, but I was just insulting the honor of your ship when the bosun decided to take the matter outside for some settlement."

It was the sort of attempted deflection one might expect from experienced non-commissioned officers trying to keep each other out of trouble with their officers (so they could get on with settling matters on their own terms). Todd had heard such attempts before, and was generally not impressed: "I wasn't speaking to you, Sergeant. Bosun, you know my expectations when we are in port."

The big Irishman was immediately chastened; it was clear that Todd was well respected by his ship's company, because there was no sign that McKenna or any of the sailors were frustrated by his intervention. Sheepish was more like it.

"I'm sorry, sir," the big Irishman immediately gave up his ground, and Todd took a heavy breath before shaking his head. "Yes, I bloody well expect you are. All of you men…" the Captain turned his eyes to his sailors. "You can do better, and I intend to see you will do so. Now whatever this was about, it stops instantly or your leave will be revoked for the duration."

With that, the Captain turned away from the bosun, surprising all the Newfoundlanders who were watching — it was expected, of course, that a British officer would flog his men for being, well, men… but this one seemed to possess enough respect to be able to scold with moral authority alone. That was worth paying attention to.

Now his attention fixed on Lady Anne, "My sincerest apologies, M'Lady. I'm sure this will not happen again."

"My apologies as well, Captain. We'll all be better friends when you come to see the Fort tomorrow."

"Sooner than that, I should hope," Todd turned away from the Viscountess and waved for his men to disperse, "Away with you now, lads. No more of this."

With a last, rather less heated glare, the bosun left Strong and the b'ys who'd assembled as an audience. Together with his shipmates, he moved back into the Hut, avoiding eye contact with a girl who was standing beside the door as he passed her. With that done, Todd offered a parting nod to her Ladyship, then departed for his ship.

"Well, that worked out," the Colour said with a grin, but when his eyes shifted back to Anne his good humor was deflated by her glare.

"Which girl?" she asked in a decidedly grumpy tone.

For two decades, Anne had been helping make sure the survivors of the Newfoundland Regiment were given all the best chances they could want... and also keeping them out of too much trouble. She and Jimmy had been forced to use a lot of clout to keep Strong out of the stockade after his run-in with the Minister of War, but it seemed no matter how much good they did, the answer to the question 'what would Mike Strong do?' usually proved a troublesome one.

Now it was the Sergeant's turn to go sheepish, "Daphne. One of the girls in the kitchen."

Anne's humorless glare turned towards the door of the Hut, and as it settled on a pretty young girl standing there, she raised her eyebrow, "Pretty, young, and making eyes at you?"

Strong's sheepishness didn't last, "That would describe many girls I'm acquainted with, M'Lady..."

"Colour," Anne's sharp riposte fought off Strong's mischievous smile before it could take command of his face, and he cleared his throat.

"Yes. Sorry, Lady Anne."

The Viscountess just had to shake her head. Strong wasn't nearly as bad as he wanted everyone to believe — she'd known him for long enough, and mothered him since she'd been the age of the girl now standing in the door, swooning over his protectiveness. Still, she had to be disapproving when his efforts to maintain his reputation led to street brawling.

"What will we do with you, Mike?" she asked eventually, shaking her head. Then she realized she'd set herself up, and just as he opened his mouth to suggest another version of that question, she held up her hand, "You tell me to ask what Mike Strong would do, I'll throw you in the harbor."

Strong just managed not to smile at that promise, "You never need to *ask*, Lady Anne. I'll do whatever you tell me to."

To any other woman, that might have come across as a line, but Anne knew her boy better. He could be as mature as a child, but when push came to shove, he was still one of the men who'd survived Waller's charge... and she knew the price he continued to pay for that day. Of the men who had lived through the assault, he was one of the few still in uniform, so as much as she could be frustrated, she was proud too.

"Go put Daphne to bed, then," was her answer. "Before the poor girl swoons herself off her feet."

Sensing that he was allowed to smile this time, Strong began to grin, then glanced back towards the door to the Hut. Sure enough, delicate Daphne was there waiting. She'd need to be walked home — her shift in the kitchen would have ended by now, and the room where she stayed alone was nearly a mile away. She didn't need an escort, because the whole way was lit by electric street lamps, but she always felt better when he was along.

Of course he wouldn't let her down...

"And be at Jimmy's office first thing in the morning," Lady Anne interrupted the Sergeant's thoughts with that instruction. "Much though it pains me to say this, we have work for you, Mike. No more motor pool."

That was rather unexpected — Strong's condemnation to work as a clerk in Fort Waller's motor pool had been part of his reprieve after the Minister of War incident. Actual work... sounded promising.

"As the your Ladyship pleases," the big Sergeant bowed, and just to make sure he was under no impressions that he was charming, Anne flicked him on his big head.

"You'll give me ulcers, Mike Strong," she shook her head and turned away.

Instantly a frown overtook the Sergeant's expression, and as she walked off he called to her, "No, M'Lady, that is *not* something Mike Strong would do!"

"Shut up, Colour," was Anne's reply, given without even looking back. It drew a laugh from the b'ys around the Sergeant, and another grin from the man himself.

Lady Anne knew how to deal with all her boys. Now, as she disappeared into the night, the audience of soldiers crowded around to pat their Sergeant on the back before heading back into the Hut to continue their games until lights out.

One handed Strong his blouse before leaving him, and the big veteran was left to accept Daphne's greeting, "Thank you, Colour Strong. You're my hero."

With a greeting like that, Mike Strong knew what to do: he took Daphne's hand and gallantly kissed it, "I've been ordered to see you to bed, by none other than the Viscountess of the Grasslands. I must not disappoint."

With a bright smile, Daphne nodded, and then with her hand wrapped up tight in his, she joined the Sergeant in the march to her rented room. But while the Colour tried never to divide his attention when escorting a woman, Anne's last words left him surprised. New work? Surely they couldn't be giving him something important to do...

The morning would tell. For this moment, he had other responsibilities.

It had to be asked: what *would* Mike Strong do?

CHAPTER VI

The uniform of a Champion had emerged with the first graduates from the Lady Emily Academy in 1935, and though many observers assumed the style had been carefully planned by someone with a great deal of power and influence, it had really developed more like a popular fashion trend — a case of hundreds of young notables trying to set themselves apart based on the their attire.

As the first-ever Champion (a title she'd never in fact possessed during the Hubrin War), Emily had always worn breeches, riding boots, a blouse and a tailored soldier's tunic — a style that suited her rather adventurous personality, but which was also highly practical in action. Skirts obviously would have done her no good when she leapt into the air, and keeping clothes closely-fitted reduced the chances that savages, her then-greatest adversary, would get a grip on her as she raced around doing them harm.

Photos of Emily from those times were still found all across the Empire — especially after her disappearance, which turned her into something of a legend — and her style had informed the fashion of many of the first classes coming out of the Academy that bore her name. Most of those early graduates had been female — girls often matured into their Champion abilities younger than the boys — so breeches and short coats naturally became the preferred style. Hundreds of young Emily-styled Ladies thus stormed onto the world scene, and immediately they caused a fashion sensation — one that quickly became centered around their coats.

Five years later, popular fashion for Champions hadn't changed, and the tradition of selecting a coat had become a rite of passage. Each Lord and Lady was obliged to choose one that reflected his or her personality, and knowing her decision lay ahead, Alex had long been making plans. However, despite getting a very early start on her first day as a Lady, the search was not going well. She could visualize the perfect coat... but, of course, it was nowhere to be found on the rack.

"You sure your heart's set on green?"

It was somewhat unique that Alex was able to bring her mother shopping with her at Mister Randsford's Coat Store — one of the few commercial operations in Jimmystown, established specifically to provide Champions with the finest coat selection. Most Champions chose by themselves, and if occasionally a foster parent did assist, the contribution was mainly notional. But as Caralynne was herself a Champion, her inherent authority to make a recommendation was greater — not that she'd override Alex's choice.

Green was the color that Alex had long thought would

be natural for her — she loved the shades of green she saw with every swim around the island, and was also partial to the way the color blended with the battle dress uniforms of the Special Service Regiment.

But Mister Randsford's store didn't have the green she wanted. There were some off shades, and a couple of options in the gentlemen's section that would have warranted extensive work with a scissors and sewing machine if she didn't want to be lost in them...

None that were quite what she was looking for.

At first she greeted that revelation with a little bit of denial, but as she moved from rack to rack once, then twice, and then a third time without seeing anything special, reality gradually crept in: "I might be losing faith."

Caralynne didn't immediately reply; her daughter's frown was deepening, so she thought it best just to let Alex continue to look until something caught her eye. It didn't help that even many of the ladies' coats were too large — Randsford naturally stocked his shop with the most common sizes for Champions, but because of the peculiarities of her origin, Alex was shorter and slimmer than most.

But surely a coat would be found to fit her — if she had to wait to have one altered, it would be a down start to her first day as a Lady.

Alex was consciously avoiding similar thoughts. A piece of cloth with some buttons hardly defined her... but the coat was one of those things about being a Champion that meant more than it ought to. She'd heard one Lady comparing it to the selection of a wedding dress, and she could understand why, though a wedding dress was worn only once, and this coat was meant to shape a lifelong identity.

So if she couldn't be green, what could young Lady Alex possibly be?

Perhaps it was fate that she was preoccupied with that question as she approached the next rack. Her attention was just beginning to drift when, amongst all the blues, reds and blacks, a white shoulder appeared. It was part of a smaller coat — one that was awkwardly stuffed between all the bigger ones around it. She sympathized instantly.

A white coat? That didn't belong in this store — no Champion with any sense would pick white for a coat, because it'd be impossible to keep clean. And it was much too small to be hanging next to the rest of the coats that surrounded it. Poor thing was in a very awkward situation.

Apparently it was her soulmate.

Reaching out, Alex shoved aside the big dark coats that were crowding her white one. By the time her fingers ran over its bright, soft fabric, she was helpless — as sure as if it was a puppy that had locked onto her with its big shiny eyes. The coat adopted her, and she adopted it.

"Found it," she blurted out the words as she ran her fingers over its shoulder strap and its big silver button. She hadn't even tried it on, but that was just a formality. There was no way it wouldn't fit.

Undoing the buttons, she pulled it off its hanger and quickly swept it up onto her shoulders, then turned for a mirror. She'd been wearing the fitted blue blouse and tight black trousers she'd always planned to pair with green. Now, as she approached her reflection, she discovered they combined just as nicely with white.

Staring at herself in the mirror, Alex discovered she'd become a Champion. The white coat made her one.

By the time Caralynne noticed her daughter had moved to the mirror, and was glowing under white fabric, Alex had already done up the buttons and folded back the double-breasted collar. She was smiling at her own reflection, and twisting and turning to make sure the coat and its tails didn't bind.

Approaching from behind, Caralynne assessed the garment and then nodded thoughtfully, "It fits very well." She then stopped right behind her daughter, their eyes meeting in the mirror, "You want to dye it?"

Alex frowned slightly, and then the coat gave her another puppy-dog stare. Those were getting disconcerting, since it was a coat, and it didn't have eyes. Just lots of shiny buttons...

"I don't know if it'd like that," she answered slowly.

Caralynne began to nod... then stopped, "Wait. What?"

Alex blinked, "I don't know if I'd like that."

Caralynne narrowed her eyes, then decided to just go with it — it was Alex's big day, after all. She said: "Well, you're the first Champion in white that I've ever heard of."

Young Lady Smith nodded, then spun slowly before the mirror one last time. No turning back: the coat had her.

"That's me," she agreed. "And I think somewhere in the world, a dry cleaner just got his wings."

That earned a laugh from Caralynne, but Alex was too fixated on her new coat to notice. She'd settled on the wardrobe that would define her first years as a Champion. But she wasn't the only one trying on clothes that morning...

A Second Lieutenant in Viscount Devlin's Own Special Service Regiment was expected to wear the battle dress of the British Army, and that suited Stephanie Shylock just fine. As much as she could make herself stylish when circumstances warranted, her upbringing on the frontier of the new world had left her little interest in ribbons, or bows, or whatever constituted the latest fashion.

Having a uniform that had been designed for utility was ideal... provided it fit. That was her morning's biggest question: would she be able to walk out of the Fort Waller Supply Office in green, or was it off to a tailor so that she didn't appear to be wearing her father's old suit? Stephanie had purchased some custom-fitted khaki shirts that she could wear instead of the uniform issue, but hiring a tailor to produce a full set of 1937-pattern Imperial Battle Dress would be a whole lot more effort, so she very much hoped the standard kit would work.

The Chief Supply Officer had initially been helping Stephanie with such uniform questions, but once they did some rough guesses as to which size would fit her, the rest of the work was handed off to his secretary Gina — helping a young lady get dressed was not something Major Percival was particularly keen on attempting, for sake of decorum.

Now Stephanie and Gina stood in a back office within the supply warehouse, a mirror propped up against the wall as they tried the high-waisted uniform pants.

"They're about an inch and a half too big on you," Gina was frowning as she pulled the trousers tight over Stephanie's waist. They were working with the slimmest-fit tall uniform they could find, but most men who stood five feet and eight inches simply couldn't have been as small as Stephanie — at least not without being too malnourished to serve. That thought prompted Gina's next suggestion: "Maybe if you start eating a lot, right now, you could grow up into it."

Stephanie smiled at the prospect, then shook her head, "Has to fit even if I'm in the field for a week without food."

Of course it did, so Gina nodded thoughtfully... then stepped behind the Regiment's newest officer and stared at her back.

As with all battle dress trousers, this particular pair had belt loops at the back that buttoned at the top of the waistband. They were about three inches apart... so what if...

"We might cross-button the straps back here. Wouldn't be able to button your trousers to your blouse, but…" Gina crouched down without finishing that sentence, and Stephanie watched patiently, holding the pants up until she suddenly felt them tighten. "How's that, child?"

It wasn't bad at all; Stephanie released the trousers' waistband and was delighted to find that they didn't fall onto her hips. Gina then planted a hand on her shoulder and turned her around, so she could look at the work in the mirror, "See, just cross-buttoned them. No need to alter a thing."

That was rather good news, so Stephanie smiled, "I was expecting more effort."

"Of course you were, because you doubted me," Gina answered with a smile, then moved over to the desk where she'd dropped the blouse and grabbed it.

Although it was officially termed a 'blouse', Stephanie would more properly have called the top half of the uniform a 'jacket', because it went on over her khaki shirt and drab green necktie. It was quite a practical garment, too — this model of uniform had been based on European skiing suits, so it was comfortable and warm, and lacked tails or flaps that would catch on the equipment and vehicles that were increasingly a part of modern soldiering.

"I've buttoned down the cuffs to the smallest size, so they shouldn't slide down over your hands," Gina continued as she opened the blouse and held it up for Stephanie. It slipped on with great ease, and then as the American girl turned back to the mirror and started buttoning up its front, she was confronted with the sudden reality that she was an officer.

Then she noticed the red diamond pips of a Second Lieutenant had even been added to the epaulets for her.

A real officer.

"It fits pretty good," Gina was suddenly blocking the mirror, tugging at the sleeves to make sure they bloused properly. "Now you brought your own boots, right? Get into those and we'll blouse your trousers."

That all sounded good, but Stephanie wasn't quite ready to budge from in front of the mirror. She was in uniform — properly in uniform — and soon she and her Champion would be off having adventures.

Stephanie Shylock couldn't keep the smile off her face for the whole rest of the fitting. Gina didn't mind.

Mike Strong was standing outside Lord Jimmy's office as he waited for the Viscount's first meeting of the day to finish. The Sergeant had no idea who was in so early — he himself had arrived at the Headquarters at 0700, which he figured would have given him plenty of time to get his orders first, but now it was passing 0930 and the door remained shut.

Not that Colour Strong minded too much. Soldiers knew how to wait, and he'd gotten especially good at it since being condemned to clerk's life in the motor pool. At least this massive Headquarters, with its ridiculous amounts of space, held plenty of things for him to look at while he stood around.

Jimmy's outer office was a particular treasure trove of photos from the old days — mostly pictures from newspapers and personal collections that dated back to 1919 and 1920. That was a time the Sergeant's mind often returned to, whether he wanted it to or not... glorious days when the Royal Newfoundland Regiment had been marching around the grasslands, trying to figure out who the Hubrin were and what they were about.

Strong had joined the regiment as a boy in 1914, and had been a private soldier with Colonel Tobin and Major Waller when they'd been shipped off first to Egypt, then Afghanistan. The latter location had taught many hard lessons; under fire from Afghan snipers, he and many of the b'ys had learned the rules of war, mostly from the Indian men they'd fought alongside.

By the time they'd been sent to the new world, and tasked with guarding Emily and Caralynne on a mysterious grasslands march, the b'ys of the RNR had been veterans, and that had served them well all through the Hubrin War.

Right until the end. Right until those blue men had revealed their lightning machine guns... or pulse cannons, as Strong had since learned to call them.

He'd been with the b'ys when they charged against

those lightning guns... when they'd all chosen to die because their loss might give the Saa dragon accompanying them — a fine engineer who everyone called Sass because her name was impossible to pronounce — the chance she needed to break through.

It had worked, but only Strong and a handful of the men who'd charged remained alive. Luck had saved them, and few had accepted their survival well. Strong himself still suffered from it more times than he let most people see... but he figured taking his own life, or living in abject misery, would have been wrong. So though he missed out on some things... family being most important amongst them... Mike Strong still made a point of laughing and loving as much as possible.

But sometimes he remembered without warning, and he found himself in a depression. The strangest cues could bring on one of those moods — an unexpected remark, sound, or even smell might remind him of his buddies who had died in the lightning. Then he'd be in darkness until his mind found a way around it, and he stopped seeing horrific pictures in his mind's eye.

Certainly not something he wanted to deal with at this particular moment, so the Sergeant closed his eyes against the photo he'd been staring at — one staged by newsmen some weeks after that deadly charge, shortly before the b'ys had left the new world to return home. Better to leave it behind, so he prepared to turn away.

When the hand landed on his shoulder, Strong half-jumped in surprise. Few men could sneak up on the wily Sergeant, even when he was distracted...

But thanks to years of frontier experience, Smith knew how to be quiet.

"Jesus... sorry... by God, Mister Smith," with practiced deftness, Strong buried his melancholy thoughts and assumed a grin as he spotted the American.

Of course Smith had been with the Newfoundlanders on the new world — he'd found them on their first march, and despite having had to leave and come back, he'd been adopted as one of their own. His presence on the rock ever since had made him well and truly one of Newfoundland's sons, and of course, he was a welcome friend to all the soldiers who'd been with Waller during the war.

Now the former-drifter nodded to the photo the Sergeant had been fixating on, "Remembering?"

Strong kept up his practiced smile, but he answered carefully, "The old days don't seem all that long ago. Wish some of the other b'ys had been around to see all this now, though."

Smith agreed with a nod, but decided not to get too involved in thinking on the dead. It wasn't that he did not respect those men... he counted them all as some of the best he'd ever known... but today's subject was more focused on the future. Hindsight wouldn't help it much.

"Are you here to see Lord Jimmy? I've been waiting a

while, but if you have something urgent, you can have first go," the Colour pressed on to matters more at hand, and Smith shook his head once, then turned his hat — which Strong only just noticed — over in his hands.

"I'm in for the same meeting as you," the American replied, and Strong responded with a thoughtful frown.

"Really? Lady Anne said there was work... you need something I can help with?"

Though Strong had never counted Smith as a close friend, he still would be pleased to work alongside the former drifter — it would be a call back to those days that had been making him maudlin, to a time when he felt more as though his work mattered.

"I do," Smith answered, and Strong's hopes spiked. But then came the continuation: "Though things are a bit more complicated. They think Emily might be back, but gone wrong. She might have killed the Champion of New York, trying to find an engineer bound for Washington."

Perhaps it wasn't right to start providing all that information without Jimmy, but Smith reckoned there wasn't much point to making Strong wait. Now the Sergeant's eyes widened in surprise, and he considered trying to speak... but Smith continued first, "Jimmy's in there with the Champions we have here. They're being sent out to protect other engineers and scientists, in case Emily tries for them."

Strong managed to nod, though he wasn't certain he

quite understood all the implications of what was being said. Emily had certainly had her troubles after Waller's death, and to be fair, even before... but she'd been a great heroine. Killing a Champion, looking for an engineer? It sounded all wrong for the first Lady to fight alongside the Newfoundlanders.

Still, if Smith was saying it, there had to be truth to it — the American didn't waste his words.

"Need help to try to track her down?" Strong reached the natural conclusion, and asked that question quietly. As one of the survivors from the old RNR, it might have made sense for Strong to join a hunting party... though men like Regimental Sergeant Major King and Regimental Sergeant Major Halloran had known Emily better.

Smith shook his head, "More important than that."

Again Strong was surprised, and as Smith considered the big Sergeant's face with his steady gaze, the American made his purpose clear: "This meeting is you and me and Jimmy. Because Caralynne is out with my daughter, choosing her coat. And because Stephanie Shylock is over at the Supply Office, getting a Lieutenant's uniform."

Both Alex and Stephanie were well known around Jimmystown — they were famous daughters of heroes from the Hubrin War, after all — and though Strong had met neither in person, he immediately realized the significance of those two pieces of news.

Of course Alex had always been expected to put on the

coat of a Champion — her only other choice for work would have been teaching at the Academy, and no one thought she'd want to do that right away. Time in the field first, and some experience, and then she could become an instructor if she liked.

But then, class sizes were growing smaller every year, as fewer savage children were being found and rescued on the new world... so perhaps there would be no teaching at all for Smith's daughter. Instead she'd have a lance of her own, along with a headstrong young American Lieutenant who happened to be a girl.

They'd need a Sergeant, Strong realized. And the only reason he could possibly be learning all of this when he was, and where he was...

"It was between you and Sergeant Cooper. But you're a better match for Alex and Stephanie," Smith knew Strong was keeping up, so he went straight to that declaration, and then he fell silent.

Strong was equally quiet — grappling with the entire notion of what he was hearing. He was to be the Sergeant of Alex's lance? There were NCOs across the Fort who would have honestly killed to secure such a post... men who'd have seen it as an opportunity for great career advancement, great glory, or if they were fools, even romance.

But Mike Strong wasn't under any such illusions: to follow Alex and Stephanie into whatever adventures lay ahead would be a staggering responsibility. They were the daughters of people who'd been on the field that fateful day — Smith, Caralynne, and the Shylock brothers had all been in the Hubrin capital when Waller had led the charge of the Newfoundlanders.

Indeed, rescuing Jimmy Devlin's assault force, along with Stephanie's father and Smith, had been Waller's purpose in ordering the final assault. That none of those people had needed rescuing proved to be a cruel twist of fate, but it didn't matter now. The reason then-Private Strong had stood up and charged into a lightning storm was to try to save them from the Hubrin and the savages.

Now Smith's daughter needed a Sergeant, and that was a responsibility that he simply could not ignore. No Newfoundlander who'd fought in 1919 or 1920 could.

As those deep and dark thoughts of obligation crossed Strong's face, Smith studied the Sergeant. Because Jimmy and Anne shared all news of their regiments with Caralynne and Smith, Alex's father knew all about the Colour's reputation — what was truth and what was invented. He knew Strong was a good soldier, and he knew what he'd done twenty years prior.

That's why it had to be Strong: because he could keep up with Alex and Stephanie on wit, and he could fight like hell for them if the day ever came that they needed it.

And with Emily perhaps gone wrong, such a day could fast arrive...

Mike Strong swallowed once, then found himself

glancing back to the pictures on the wall.

"Well," he said, "you actually managed to make me speechless, Mister Smith. I mean, of course I'm honored to do it, but I wish I could figure something better than that to say."

Smith didn't know why a man would need to say anything better than that he was honored, but understood that some were always keen to try.

"No need to say a certain thing. I know you're the man for it," was the former-drifter's answer, and Strong took a breath.

"I'll take care of them."

Smith nodded, "And they'll look out for you."

Strong imagined there'd be a lot of that too, though he wouldn't admit as much. A quiet descended over both men as they considered all the implications of their words. Eventually the door to Jimmy's office opened, letting out Champions — Lord Grey, Lord Kyle, Lady Sheldon, Lady Winter, and a half-dozen others. They were off to the Torbay Airport, where they'd board skycruisers bound for points around the Empire — places they could go to protect engineers and scientists against whatever danger they faced, Emily or otherwise.

The Viscount himself was last out the door, and he immediately spotted his old comrades-in-arms, "Smith, Colour, sorry it took so long!"

Crossing the oversized outer office to the corner where

the two men stood, Jimmy clapped his hands together, "Well Mike, I have a bit of a surprise for you…"

He paused as soon as he saw the Sergeant's serious face, "Wait. Smith told you everything, didn't he?"

Strong blinked, looked at Smith, then nodded.

Smith shrugged, "Reckoned it'd save time."

Jimmy narrowed his eyes, "Of course. I was just looking forward to dragging it out for as long as possible, to make him suffer for his lecherous ways."

"Oh," Smith answered. "I didn't do that."

"No," Lord Devlin observed. "Well, that's alright. Let's get your paperwork sorted, Colour. Oh, but I still can't promote you. That's the deal with the Minister…"

Together with Smith and Strong, the Viscount of the Grasslands headed back into his office. The newest Champion's team was quickly assembling — perhaps just in time…

CHAPTER VII

"I've heard that your godfather is a gunfighter. Is that right, Lieutenant?"

Stephanie was going to have to get used to being addressed by her rank — Lord Jimmy's regiment was famously informal, but most of its NCOs would still be inclined to greet her that way. Now she nodded to the Sergeant who was collecting items for her from behind the armory counter.

"Cameron Kard," she said. "He taught me to shoot as soon as I was taller than my pa's rifle."

The old-timer smiled at those words — confirmation of the stories he'd heard from time to time over the years about the fine American girl who had designs on being an officer. Rumors were always common among soldiers, and in Jimmystown they were nearly as good as currency — *buy me a drink and I'll tell you what I heard about Stephanie Shylock!*

"Must have been some young," the Sergeant finally returned to the counter in front of his newest customer with an armful of kit.

"Very young," Stephanie favored him with a smile. "Pa's rifle was a carbine."

"Aha!" the old b'y laughed, then took a step back. "Alright, that's all your kit, including magazines and a box of ammo. You have a look through, I'll go and get the piece for you."

With a nod, Stephanie watched the Sergeant disappear back into the Fort Waller armory. With her uniform fitting smartly, she was now being issued her sidearm: a Browning Hi-Power pistol that would accompany her wherever she went. The holster was already in front of her, so as she waited for the gun to arrive Stephanie quickly looked it over, then considered the magazines and the box of 9mm rounds that had been provided.

She could draw more ammunition whenever she needed, though if she wanted additional magazines for the pistol — and she figured she would — she'd have to acquire those privately. That suited her fine...

"Here it is. Shiny and new," the Sergeant reappeared with those words, carrying a box that looked suspiciously special — as though he'd pulled it out just for the girl officer who was such a breath of fresh air in his stuffy day.

"Thank you, Sergeant," Stephanie smiled as the box was set down and opened before her.

The pistol was black and indeed shiny — its metal frame had been coated with an enamel to resist corrosion, so it lacked the dull metal finish she'd been accustomed to on other guns of its kind.

Picking it up, she locked back its slide and proceeded

to check to see it was unloaded, then turned it over in her hands.

"They say it's the best pistol of its kind," the Sergeant commented with a smile — clearly he just liked talking to her, which Stephanie found rather sweet. "I remember the Webleys we used to have back in the old days. I think Lord Jimmy still's got one... but I hear these are better..."

Stephanie shrugged at that, then inserted one of the empty magazines into the pistol and released its slide, "I learned to shoot with a Smith and Wesson revolver first, but then Uncle Kard got me going with the Colt 1911. Said it was probably the way of the future, he just didn't like it as much for himself."

Turning in a safe direction, Stephanie raised the pistol with a straight arm, making sure the sights were level with her eye. The grip was comfortable, and it pointed well — not unlike the 1911, which had been designed for Colt by the same man, John Browning, who'd created this Hi-Power.

"This one is the regimental model," the Sergeant was pleased the conversation was going two directions, so he offered a bit more detail. "Spur hammer... the Champions' guns were made by John Inglis and have ring hammers. They's all got the magazine safety, but we tune up the triggers to make sure they're good and crisp for you. Safety on the slide too..."

Lowering the pistol again, Stephanie re-confirmed that it was empty and then pointed it safely away from the Sergeant, thumbed back the hammer and squeezed the trigger. The magazine safety that came standard on these pistols — meant to keep them from firing without a magazine seated — was notorious for ruining trigger pull. This one, however, was very crisp, and her smile grew, "Very nice trigger job. Your work?"

"I wish," the old Sergeant grinned. "Were it mine, I wouldn't be here taking signatures the whole day."

Satisfied with her sidearm, Stephanie laid it back down on the counter, but kept smiling at the man, "Well I'm glad it's not yours, because I wouldn't want anyone else here to get me sorted out."

Getting an old soldier to turn a little red was no mean feat, but Stephanie managed it with that. She never minded being sweet to a kindly old-timer, and as his cheeks heated up, he found himself at a loss for words. She therefore offered him a little help, "So I'm going to sign somewhere?"

He nodded, "Right on..."

Turning to the back counter, he found the necessary ledger books, collected them and then laid them before her, along with a pen. He then pointed to the relevant lines, and she inscribed her name with flowing letters.

"There," she said, pushing the ledgers back towards him. Then she paused, looked conspiratorially over her shoulder to make sure no one else was in the office, and leaned forward. "Now, what would you recommend if I needed more magazines for this fine pistol?"

Following the new officer's lead, the old-timer looked conspiratorially around the office too. It was a quiet morning so they were truly alone.

"Well," said he, "stuff does go missing here from time to time."

Stephanie turned her head a little so she could look at him slightly sideways, then spoke a little conspiratorially, "Only if it's no trouble."

"Oh my dear, I can't hardly count anyway," he assured her, turning around and collecting a box from a low shelf. He then held it out over the counter and made a point of looking away.

It wasn't really stealing, of course — it was hardly as though Stephanie was going to sell the magazines. She just had to be certain she had enough, because she was terribly fond of shooting.

Once her pockets were suitably full, she cleared her throat and looked away, casually rocking up and down on the balls of her feet.

"That feels lighter than I thought, but I must be off," the Sergeant said with a grin as he replaced the box on the shelf, then turned back to his honored guest. "But with that, I'm sad to say you're all set up. I have no more claim to you, Lieutenant."

"Aw," was Stephanie's answer, though she was already collecting the official parts of her kit so she could take everything away. That done, she nodded to the Sergeant, stepped back from the counter... then stopped and stepped back in his direction again.

With a quick nod, she encouraged the fellow to lean forward, as though she needed to whisper something, and as soon as he did she kissed him on the cheek, "Thanks Sergeant."

Well if he'd been red before, he was crimson when Stephanie leaned back. She turned away from the counter and made for the door, stopping just before she opened it to offer a parting tease, "Probably shouldn't tell anyone you were kissed by a Lieutenant, eh Sergeant?"

"No sir, ma'am," was his answer, and with a grin and a quick wave, she departed.

The old-timer Sergeant planted his elbow on the counter and rested his chin in his hand. It was a strange world in which girls were becoming officers in the army... but he figured he'd find a way to cope.

Alex knew the Academy's Champion training course as well as she knew the Browning Hi-Power she'd been issued. After years of schooling with both her mother and the other Academy instructors, she was entirely accustomed to moving and shooting, to scaling obstacles and dropping safely from heights that would kill most ordinary people.

Because of her familiarity with all of these things, she supposed standing at the beginning of this course should not have been any different today. But it was, because she was wearing her white coat.

"The line is clear — whenever you're ready, Lady Alex," the range officer called out to her, and she nodded to him in thanks. Then she set off.

Two miles of difficult obstacles set upon a treacherous piece of Newfoundland terrain, the assault course was designed to make sure Champions going out into the world were prepared for anything they might run into. Somehow Alex doubted that every conceivable obstacle could be installed in just two miles... but it was still a challenge.

Starting up the first slope as fast as she could manage, she imagined that she appeared to onlookers as a white blur. She was slightly bent at the waist, her Browning held straight out in front of her but angled down towards the ground, her shoulders squared so that she was squarely facing her direction of travel.

The first leg of the course was up a slope of loose rock, and as she deftly planted her feet around the less stable points, she kept her eyes sweeping from left to right, then back again. That was a technique Smith brought to the Champion curriculum: as a drifter on the new world, Alex's father had known that if a person stared too long at one scene, he or she could miss something obviously out of place. Scanning back and forth made it easier to spot something that didn't belong—

Alex lined up her Browning on a target just as it began to pop up out of the rocks, then put two shots through its 'head' without missing a step.

One more target popped out from behind concealment before she reached the top of the slope, and it fell with equal ease. Then Alex crested the rise, spent a second considering the steep, densely-treed drop before her, and jumped.

The descent was close to vertical — perhaps seventy-five or eighty degrees. Making her way down such an incline was mostly a matter of controlled falling; she moved her feet quickly and leapt from crooked tree to crooked tree all the way down.

As she dropped, another target popped out of the slanted woods — like the trees, it seemed to grow sideways out of the near-cliff that she was falling down. Two more rounds from her Browning defeated it, and then Alex deftly returned her attention to her descent. The bottom was coming fast, and as she caught sight of the muddy bog that dominated it, she did feel a pang of regret about her white coat.

Newfoundland bogs were known for stealing boots right off the feet of wearers, and muddying whatever attire one happened to have on, but if she was careful…

Spotting a bigger tree sticking more or less sideways out of the bottom of the slope, Alex tapped her toes to the ground and changed the direction of her descent. Using her free hand, she got a grip on one of that evergreen's branches and levered herself up onto its trunk.

The tree was at least five or six meters tall, looking as

ratty and disheveled as most Newfoundland vegetation did. Checking her balance, she started working her way up its trunk, which was actually only reaching upwards at a thirty-five degree angle because it was growing sideways out of the slope.

One foot after another, carefully keeping her balance as she ascended without her hands, Alex made it to the top of the old pine. It groaned under her — seeming not to appreciate how light she was — so she knew she'd have to leap from it in a hurry. She just had to gauge how far.

The bog here changed regularly based on rainfall — how wide, how deep, how muddy was always a surprise. Today, the relatively dry August had left it eminently passable, with a deep layer of mud for only twenty yards or so. Assessing its narrowest point, Alex chose what appeared to be a sensible landing area, then leapt.

As usual, her timing and distance estimates were good; covering the thirty yards through the air to a rock on the far side, she watched the tepid water, grasses, and mudholes pass below her. Then she landed without so much as a wobble.

A target popped out of the woods as soon as she touched down, so she gave that poor silhouette of a savage two more shots from her Browning, then leapt forward again.

The bog had been in the base of a valley, so now she needed to scale the other side. It was an equally difficult tree-covered slope, but ascending in such conditions was a completely different challenge.

Leaping up from tree to tree, keeping her eyes moving regularly as she shot a couple of targets and always watched where to put her feet, she made the climb in a few minutes, then found herself in a clearing at the crest of a ridge. This was always her favorite part: the sea view from this high vantage point was incredible. Pausing for a moment to catch her breath, and drawing a kerchief from her coat pocket to dab her glistening brow, Alex smiled out into the freshening breeze that was gliding off the blue water. She was within easy reach of her beloved ocean, and she felt a pang of longing — she'd have loved a swim just now.

But today was about work, and as she thought that, the next two targets popped from the trees simultaneously. Alex was her father's daughter... and her mother's daughter too. Having been raised by such fine shooters, the young Lady had no trouble laying two rounds into each invader. Knowing her Browning was dry after that, she slid out its magazine and introduced another before hurrying on. There was another mile to cover through the Newfoundland woods — even a cliff to scale — and then she had to come back.

All while keeping her coat spotless...

CHAPTER VIII

Aside from being the matriarch of all Newfoundland's soldiers, Lady Anne also served as the resident diplomat at Jimmystown. As the Viscountess, she commanded sufficient authority and notoriety to be an appropriate host for all manner of guests, and by keeping people like visiting Royal Navy Captains occupied, she made certain Jimmy had time to do all the paperwork involved with running Champion operations.

She was also able to gather intelligence without anyone realizing. Indeed, she'd established a network of covert sources around both worlds — past guests of Jimmystown who were quite happy to stay in touch with the charming and refined Lady Devlin, only sometimes realizing how much information they were handing over to her, whether she was supposed to have it or not.

To call Anne a spymaster would have been too much; she preferred to think of herself as working in hospitality, and indeed, her son George had joined her in managing that portfolio. It was vitally important work, and on this particular morning, it meant she was showing Captain Percy Todd around Fort Waller.

Of course, a destroyer Captain was not the sort of man Anne particularly needed to grill for information — unlike political officials from continental European countries, or industrialists from the United States, he was more a guest in the traditional sense. Nevertheless, Anne knew it was wise to make sure he got the best possible impression of the Champions' home base.

Which wasn't very hard, because even on an off day the Fort was an impressive place.

And this wasn't an off day.

"Very relaxed air about the place, I must say," Todd observed as they strode down one of the Fort's many paths. Soldiers were passing by at regular intervals, none of them seemingly in a rush, though none dawdling either.

With a nod, Anne agreed, "We've kept to the spirit of the old RNR here. I know Jimmy thinks that's important... everyone is expected to deliver the very best results, and if they don't that's frowned upon. But if they do, and I must say that's much more common, then things don't need to be quite so taut."

It was an interesting approach, and Todd nodded, "I suppose it's not dissimilar to making sure you run a happy ship. Discipline when needed, but you spare the punishments until they're warranted... and hand them down without mercy when they are."

Something like that, Anne supposed, though she could hardly imagine her husband disciplining any of his b'ys to the extents of military law. For all he'd done and seen, Jimmy had never been a particularly violent man. Perhaps that was one of the reasons why so many of his officers and men went out of their way to make sure the Special Service Regiment was outstanding, and why there were so few problems with the current Royal Newfoundland Regiment.

But then, of course, the Champions were always around too. Schooled from childhood to give their best without question, they set a stunning example that most of the fighting men in Jimmystown worked hard to match. It helped that those who didn't meet the high standards were reassigned; one of the benefits of being an elite base was the ability to ship off the real riffraff.

Anne knew all this — had been part of the team that created the culture in Jimmystown — but she wasn't inclined to volunteer everything to Captain Todd, "A good comparison, I think."

The Captain nodded, and together they continued down the path, the sound of gunshots making it clear they were nearing a training range.

There weren't too many guns firing when they arrived; most of the shooting benches were unoccupied, but the lane nearest their approach did have a shooter, and the sight of that person obliged Todd to stop.

"What is this, fancy dress?" he asked immediately, then fell silent as he realized he probably shouldn't have blurted out his question so casually.

Anne's eyebrow went up but she managed to contain a smile as she folded her arms, "Not at all, Captain. I believe that is our newest Second Lieutenant, Stephanie Shylock."

Sure enough, it was indeed Stephanie standing at the bench, having just finished loading five of her magazines in preparation for what her godfather would have affectionately called 'some gunplay'. Sixteen rounds fit into each of the Browning's magazines — double what she could load into a Colt 1911, even when she kept a full magazine and one in the chamber. Filling her illicitly-acquired haul had emptied almost an entire box.

But soon all that lead would be traveling down her pistol's barrel, and with that in mind, she slid home the first magazine, racked the slide to load a round into the chamber, and prepared to open fire.

Anne managed to interrupt in time: "Good morning, Stephanie!"

Blinking in surprise, the young Lieutenant looked towards the new arrivals — being certain, of course, to keep her Browning pointed safely down range. Recognizing the Viscountess, Stephanie smiled brightly, "Lady Anne! How do I look?"

To Percy Todd, that question sounded awfully like it should have come from a silly girl playing dressup, and Anne could almost feel his scowl as she closed the distance to the shooting bench, "The battle dress suits you. Fit properly?"

Of course that was why Stephanie had asked — Anne

would appreciate the good fortune of finding a uniform that basically fit her off the shelf. But as she nodded, her gaze shifted to the Royal Navy Captain in his dress blues, and she got a slight chill. Seemed a bit of a traditionalist, and he probably had no idea why a young woman was in uniform... or worse, had Lieutenant pips on her shoulder.

Before she could react to that impression, Anne made another observation, "They issuing more magazines with officer pistols now?"

Stephanie's eyes darted back to the Lady, and found a wicked smile was on Anne's face. Of course the Viscountess knew every detail of operations on the base, and now the American girl felt her cheeks start to go red. Anne halted that with a shake of her head, "Oh no, I must be mistaken. Never you mind."

They locked eyes, and Stephanie swallowed and tried to recover her smile.

"You're serving in what capacity, Lieutenant?" Todd's question erased any doubts of his disapproval, so Anne intervened first.

"She's commanding the lance for our newest Champion, Captain Todd. Am I assuming correctly that you don't approve of a woman in uniform?"

Stephanie's eyes widened slightly and jumped back to the Viscountess at that sharp question, and Todd's gaze shifted to his host as well. He hadn't expected to be called out so directly by a Lady, but now that he had been, he was determined not to back down, "Seems unnecessary to me, for a woman to be put in such a situation."

"Even our Champions?" Anne was still smiling as she questioned the Captain, and Stephanie enjoyed the slight look of discomfort that crossed the man's face.

"No *ordinary* woman, I should have said."

Anne considered the answer thoughtfully, then nodded once and glanced back to Stephanie, "Well I could make the point that you're not terribly ordinary, Stephanie. But I'm inclined to argue on the principle that even an ordinary woman should be allowed to do whatever she pleases. If you don't mind pretending to be ordinary while I do."

"By all means," Stephanie bowed slightly, her smile reviving more naturally now that the magazine scare was over.

"Very kind of you," Anne turned back to Todd. "Well Captain, I might remind you that under this slight veneer of civility, I did start my life as a maid. I rather think any woman can do what she pleases, so long as she's willing to work to whatever ends are necessary to be capable of the duty. For myself, I had to learn how to be diplomatic in the face of rude questions. But now look at me."

It was a pointed counter to *Inglefield's* skipper, and coming from a Viscountess with such standing as Anne possessed, it did put him back on his heels. Nevertheless, he was not inclined to abandon his cause casually: "I would never cast doubt on your own accomplishments, M'Lady, but the arena of warfare is rather unforgiving."

Quite an interesting tack to take while standing at a shooting bench. Stephanie was awfully tempted to hand her brand new pistol over to see how the Captain fared with the weapon... but she didn't want to risk him breaking it. Instead she'd simply have to show her own talents.

"May I get on with my practice, Lady Anne?" she asked, and admittedly it wasn't too subtle.

Anne nodded, "I think you'll have a very interested audience, Stephanie, thank you."

That sounded fine, so with a smile, the American girl with the gunfighter for a godfather turned back towards the paper rings she'd posted downrange. Facing the target squarely, she sunk into a shooting crouch, raised her right arm at the shoulder, aligned her sights, and opened fire.

Todd's eyes shifted back and forth from target to shooter with every shot — and since Stephanie emptied the magazine at a pace that would have done Cameron Kard proud, he was barely able to keep track.

One-handed, she emptied all sixteen rounds from her first magazine, and at twenty yards not a single shot strayed outside the ten-inch ring.

Straightening slowly, Stephanie thumbed the release, pulled the exhausted magazine free, and laid her warm pistol down on the bench. It did shoot like a dream — the trigger was much crisper than she'd dared hope, with no signs at all of the magazine safety disrupting the pull. The recoil was different than she was accustomed to with a 1911, but altogether the gun was quite controllable — with a bit of time she was sure she'd be able to shrink her grouping.

Before that happened, though, she'd have to find a polite way of telling the Royal Navy Captain that he could do no better, and that gentlemen really shouldn't question ladies... particularly frontier girls who tended to be headstrong when someone implied they weren't fit for the duties they held.

Perhaps fortunately, any such attempt to assail a much-superior officer (in the presence of a Viscountess) was interrupted by a sudden unleashing of gunfire from the other side of the bench.

Spinning in surprise, and preparing to tell off whoever ever had snuck up to shoot her prized gun, Stephanie found herself staring at her beloved best friend, in a similar shooting crouch to the one she'd just abandoned.

And wearing a white coat.

Alex was shooting her own Browning — it was clearly a different gun because its hammer was a barbed ring instead of a spur — and smiling with a slight squint as she looked down range at her target...

But more much importantly, her coat was *white*.

It took fewer than twenty seconds for the Champion's magazine to run dry, and as her pistol's slide locked back to prove it was empty, Alex lowered it and straightened with a frown, "How do you always beat me at twenty yards? Had at least three fliers there…"

Stephanie knew her friend was saying that out loud for Todd's benefit — to start a conversation in which she, the Champion, pointed out that her ordinary friend was by far the more accomplished gunwoman. But putting the Captain in his place suddenly seemed less important.

"Why are you wearing white? You said green. I found green nail polish and everything."

Alex frowned, looked down at her sparkling coat — still pristine — and then turned her eyes up again. She was about to answer when she managed to count the number of loaded magazines on the shooting bench: "How'd you get so many magazines already? I was planning to steal my extras tonight."

This time Stephanie found herself entirely unashamed: "I kissed the Sergeant. But don't tell Lady Anne, or she's libel to spread that rumor and I'll have to kiss every man in the Fort."

"Aha," Alex nodded, then added: "Everyone starting with Captain Todd of the destroyer *Inglefield*, who thinks you're not fit for the uniform."

And with that, both Alex and Stephanie turned on the Briton with wide-eyed stares, that were probably more creepy than menacing. Todd quickly found himself slightly hotter under the collar than he'd expected.

"Forgive me being rude, Captain, but I did overhear you on my way here from the assault course, and I do fear you were underestimating my very best friend. Whatever your politics on the issue of suffrage, I suggest you don't doubt Stephanie Shylock, the daughter of my father's dear friends Vonn and Miranda Shylock. Niece of Bo Shylock. Goddaughter of the *gunman* Cameron Kard."

By this time Anne had simply stepped back out of the line of fire, so Todd took both barrels of ice with Alex's sharp words. It didn't help that he started to recognize the names of Stephanie's family as soon as they were recited for him: names that had joined the likes of Earp and Doc Holiday as legends of the American frontier.

Silence settled over the group after Alex's speech, and deciding it was best for diplomacy to cut some of the tension, Anne leaned slightly in the young Champion's direction: "We were actually going to make the argument about women being allowed to do whatever they wanted, even if they weren't quite so special as Stephanie."

Alex opened her mouth in surprise, then turned to Todd with a horrified gaze, "Oh I've ruined it. I'm so sorry! Captain, please forget everything I said."

At this point the navy man was ready to disengage, so he simply shook his head, "I… don't mention it. Lady Anne, I think I've been sufficiently raked here. Perhaps I'll take my leave?"

Victory was sweet, but of course Anne knew it would be impolitic to let a Royal Navy Captain sulk away after being bested by a couple of girls. Turning towards Todd, she smiled brightly and held out her hand, "Not at all, Captain. I promise this is just the beginning of your humiliation."

The way she said it was somehow almost inviting — Anne truly had learned the game of manipulation — and as she led Todd away, both Alex and Stephanie were surprised to hear him laugh at something she said.

"We're winning battles already," Alex declared as she laid her empty Browning on the bench beside her friend's.

"I totally had him handled."

"Aha, you would have hoarded all the fun for yourself!" Alex shot back, then moved around the bench to re-count the number of magazines. "So who's this Sergeant, and if I kiss him on the cheek, you think I can get more magazines?"

Stephanie smiled at her friend and shrugged, "If we both kissed him at the same time, one on each cheek, he might pass out and give us the run of the armory."

That sounded like a plan, so Alex puckered her lips as if to kiss, then tapped them a couple of times to check to make sure they were functioning properly. Satisfied they could do the job, she nodded seriously, "I am ready."

"I'll bet you are," Stephanie's smile grew. "But what about the white coat?"

Seriousness evaporating, Alex turned slightly sheepish, "It sort of followed me home."

Stephanie's eyebrow climbed at that, and then she folded her arms disapprovingly. Unable to cope with the resulting glare, the young Champion tried to bolster her defense, "It gave me the puppy-dog eyes. Really. I couldn't resist."

Of course the American Lieutenant had to point out the obvious: "It's a coat. And you and I both know coats don't have eyes. Or puppies."

"But it has lots of shiny buttons," Alex explained, and then made a show of pointing to a couple of them. "And — and — buttons are round, like eyes. So basically it's the same thing."

It was difficult to argue with such logic, and recognizing that, Stephanie simply shook her head, "I'm not getting any other nail polish. When I wear green it'll be your fault that we don't match."

Alex frowned, "I've never seen you wear nail polish. I thought you were just making that up."

Stephanie scowled, "It was special, for us. I was going to do it so we could match. Now it's ruined."

She sounded awfully wounded when she said that — no really, very heartbroken. Seriously.

And then her smile broke through, and Alex's did too.

"They're going to have a hell of a time finding a Sergeant who can handle us," the Lieutenant said.

Hand flashing up in warning, the Champion scolded her friend: "Don't say that, you'll curse us!"

But both girls knew it'd take a mighty strong curse to match their natural madness. Very *strong* indeed...

How unfortunate.

CHAPTER IX

Though the Saa dragons had not provided the British Empire and the United States with all of the tools available to their advanced science, they had been only too happy to give their human allies some machinery that was nearly magical by the measures of Earth physics. The skycruisers — two pairs of powerful heavier-than-air ships that resembled seagoing warships, but which could of course fly — were part of this exchange.

None of these machines were armed, but then they had no reason to be; they were capable of flight into the farthest reaches of Earth's atmosphere, and could accelerate to many times the speed of sound; no human weapon yet devised could hope to touch them.

The upcoming Snapdragon fighter planes were the first man-made vehicles that would have the ability to cruise with them at some of these fantastic speeds and altitudes, which was undoubtedly why the mysterious attacker in New York had been after the plans... but for now, the British Empire relied on the Spitfire for its air defense.

A couple of Spits were flying orbits over the Torbay Airport when Jimmy Devlin hopped out of his staff rover just inside the secure field's gate. Looking up at those elegant planes, the Viscount took a moment to smile — he still recalled when a mad Englishman called Carstairs had tried dueling Hubrin aircruisers in fabric-covered biplanes. At least the Spits looked like they'd have a fighting chance in a similar engagement.

But it wasn't the Spits he'd come to see. He'd sent out his two skycruisers that morning to deliver Champions to defend important persons across Canada and Britain, and the first craft was due back any moment.

"There's *Skipper Miller,* sir," accompanying Devlin was Regimental Sergeant Major Halloran of the Special Service Regiment, a gray-haired old b'y who had been alongside Jimmy back in Afghanistan, and again on the grasslands.

Now the veteran soldier pointed up to a dark shape growing rapidly as it raced towards Torbay from the west. There was no visible way to tell that particular ship, *Major Herbert Miller*, apart from its brother, *Major George Tucker*, but the latter ship had gone east over the Atlantic with Lady Winter and Lord Kyle. This ship was coming from the direction of Canada, so Halloran made the natural — and correct — assumption about its identity.

"They made good time," the Viscount said to his trusted old Sergeant, then started striding along the paved road that led from the gate down towards the large military airfield. Torbay was both a military and civilian airport, but because two Saa-built machines were constantly stationed there, the army side was especially advanced, and especially protected.

Passing guards from the Newfoundland Regiment as he led the way towards the ship's designated landing spot, Jimmy wondered how the deliveries had gone. They'd provided little warning to the engineers at the University of Toronto's Saa School that they were soon to be protected by Champions. It was hard to imagine anyone would object to being under such powerful guard, but some academic-types could be unpredictably prickly...

Bad luck for them if they were. At least the Canadian Prime Minister had been agreeable, though since Alain Lapointe was a friend of the Newfoundlanders, that agreement had been a given.

"Are the Yanks flying around Champions too?" that question came from Halloran as the pair arrived beside one of the massive hangers that provided shelter for the skycruisers, and all Jimmy could do was shrug.

"Don't know yet. They should, but that doesn't mean much..." was his answer, and Halloran shook his head.

"Figures."

The United States Regiment of Champions was the official counterpart of Lord Jimmy's Own, and though its mandate was similar to that of the Special Service Regiment, it rarely seemed to follow in its British counterpart's footsteps. As far as most of the officers and veterans in Jimmystown were concerned, that was a mistake... and not just because prideful soldiers often thought less of their peers from other services.

No, there had been a demonstrable record of poor management of the US Regiment, largely because of the political aspirations of those who always managed to get control of it. Where Lord Jimmy had been a constant and unwavering figure at the top of the Special Service Regiment, the Americans had lacked a single heroic figure who could assume the mantle of patriarch of their Champion program. It seemed to change hands after every election, being taken over by the latest wise man who saw it as a prestige appointment.

Of course, the Americans did have at least one man... indeed, one regiment... that anyone outside their borders would eagerly have pointed to as being fit to provide leadership to such an elite force. Unfortunately, the 25th United States Infantry had been condemned to serve only as guards for that nation's Champion Institute, and their Colonel Adams hadn't been promoted since 1922.

All because he and his men were black.

But that sour thought was no good for the moment; as much as Jimmy lamented the poor treatment of the buffalo soldiers he'd twice fought alongside on the new world, he had to focus on the concerns he could in some way impact — namely the defense of the Empire's secrets.

Skipper Miller was named for one of the Newfoundland Regiment's two Majors on the day of the charge, and as it floated over Torbay's field, its massive dark hull looked slightly more sinister than its namesake ever had.

"Here it comes..." Halloran warned in a low tone, putting one hand on his head to make sure his beret didn't go flying.

Jimmy mirrored the action, securing his own beret just as the ship's landing thrusters fired, guiding the destroyer-sized vessel safely to the tarmac. As the big machine's engines started to wind down, the landing ramps at its bow and stern began to lower, and the Viscount nodded to his RSM, "Let's see how that went."

With a nod, Halloran joined his longtime officer on a march down to the landing slot, just in time to see the Brigadier of the Special Service Regiment emerge from the bow ramp.

Shawn Kennedy had been a Lieutenant with the Newfoundland Regiment during the Hubrin War, and now he remained at Jimmy's right hand, helping manage the many-headed and massive Champions Regiment (which, were it more traditionally organized, might have constituted a large infantry division). Putting his beret on his head as he reached the bottom of the ramp, the Brigadier turned towards Devlin immediately and advanced with a shake of his head.

"Scientists can be a strange bunch, Jimmy," was his greeting, and the Viscount answered with a smile.

"Not happy to have guards?"

"Not happy to be interrupted. I'm pretty sure they

don't care that Grey and the rest are watching after them,
but they took awful exception to me costing them twenty
minutes of work while I explained the danger," Kennedy
answered, slowing as he, Jimmy and Halloran all came
together at the edge of the tarmac.

"Takes all kinds, I suppose," was Jimmy's answer, and
Kennedy shrugged.

The scientists now under guard were some of the
Empire's finest minds, all centralized at the Saa School
of Engineering at the University of Toronto. Despite the
name, they were mostly tasked with reverse-engineering the
technology humans had captured from the Hubrin on the
new world — the Saa provided guidance and assistance,
but insisted that human scientific knowledge be grown to a
certain level before they started handing over new principles
and machines that could lead to planet-wide destruction if
some ignorant fellow accidentally hit the wrong switch.

Both the British and American governments had agreed
to the gradual introduction of such technology over the
coming decades, largely because the machines that the Saa
were already willing to hand over — namely the skycruisers
— were, along with the Champions, more than enough to
ensure Anglo-American hegemony on both worlds. Getting
to the point of space-faring warships would be brilliant, but
it would also be expensive. So there was no hurry... at least
not for the moment.

Jimmy always wondered how long the patience of those

two governments would hold if an actual threat appeared to either of them... hopefully the New York attack wasn't the first shot in a new mess.

"Anything happen while I was away?" Kennedy's next question interrupted Devlin's expository musing, and the Viscount paused before shrugging.

"Well, today is Stephanie Shylock's first as an officer."

Kennedy's eyebrow climbed, "Oh that's good. I've been wanting gray hair."

"We're putting Mike Strong with her and Alex," Jimmy added, and Kennedy's other eyebrow went up.

"I think that's going to lead to... some..."

The Brigadier trailed off, but knowing Mike Strong pretty well, Halloran picked up: "Really bad dialogue."

That drew a laugh from both Kennedy and Devlin — the ex-Colour Sergeant's determination to have his own catchphrase was pretty legendary in Jimmystown — and then the Viscount took a breath and shook his head.

"We'll keep them close for now. Which is just as well, because I've just sent all my other Champions away. Might be time for us to consider a permanent reserve."

With that he turned and gestured back towards his rover; now that the scientists were secure, they had much work to do in trying to imagine where the attacker had come from, and where she might be found again.

That question in mind, Devlin, Kennedy and Halloran started back to Headquarters.

• • •

Being in his mid-twenties, Lord Maxwell Grey was one of the senior Champions in the Special Service Regiment. One of very few boys in the first class through Lady Emily's Academy, he'd become something of a celebrity upon his graduation — the dashing hero every society mother hoped their daughter could woo, and the man whom boys wished they could grow up to be.

Grey took it all in stride. He'd been brought up properly by good adopted parents, and had natural leadership qualities that made certain he earned the respect he was given. His recent posting to Hong Kong had been a success, and he'd even learned some tricks from Chinese boxers — a fierce bunch whose unique style for punching and kicking had drawn his notice.

Perhaps some of the techniques he'd adopted from them would serve him if Emily, or whoever the villain was, arrived in Toronto.

Because of the danger to the Saa School of Engineering, it was Grey who had been posted to the campus — along with Lord Powell, Lady Pierce, and Lady Baker. Just four Champions to watch the entire school and its complement of engineers and scientists might have seemed insufficient, but with many of those important men living in a special residence on the University of Toronto's campus, it was manageable.

They just needed to be careful, and vigilant.

Because of his relative notoriety, there was little chance of Grey's presence going unnoticed, so he made no attempt to cover his (entirely appropriate) gray peacoat as he strode around the campus in the late afternoon of a weekday. He wanted to be seen — wanted Emily, should she arrive, to know that a Champion was present. Perhaps she'd even make the mistake of openly doing battle with him.

Though she'd proved a match for Steele in New York, that fellow had been unprepared. Grey's Browning was in his coat pocket, and his senses were heightened with every passing student and professor. He also had backup.

Lady Pierce was a younger Champion, just in her early twenties, but she had proved herself most talented indeed. Having shed her coat for the sake of anonymity, she was following Grey at a distance, watching to be sure that he had help if a challenge appeared.

In the meantime, Lady Baker was moving around inside the school, and Lord Powell was on the building's roof. The four lances that had joined their Champions on this mission were arrayed around that building in a casual cordon as well. Taken together, the arrangements on this campus were more than the likes of Emily could overcome...

If the danger truly was from Lady Emily, and indeed, if she was even nearby.

That was the question which compelled the Lord to stop again. He was walking nearly 300 yards from the Saa School building, looking for any indication that something was out of the ordinary.

Some students around tried not to notice him, but many stared or smiled. He nodded back, or waved to them, but made certain his expression clarified his need not to be interrupted. Champions at work were not to be disturbed.

Something felt wrong to Grey, but he couldn't quite identify what. His instincts, if he were permitted to consider such things, were hinting at danger. But perhaps that was just anxiety… perhaps he was just too concerned about this most threatening duty.

Thrusting his hands into his pockets, the Champion made sure his grip closed properly around his Browning, then he slowly turned in place. He spotted Lady Pierce under the shade of a Norway maple, some forty yards away. Her hands were in the pockets of her breeches as she waited in a similarly casual fashion.

Turning further he considered the path he'd come down, but there was nothing out of the ordinary there. Finally he looked back towards the school building itself, some 300 yards distant…

And he stopped dead.

Halfway between himself and the school stood a caped figure. It was an unusual fashion choice for a campus in August; most of the summer students were wearing their normal suits or skirts, but none were in academic gowns.

The cape pooled at the ground, and with its hood up, it was pointed at the top. Barely more than a pyramid of cloth at this distance, but Grey knew the implications. His heart pounded, and he instantly began to crouch, drawing his Browning from his pocket.

The cape didn't move. Perhaps the wearer hadn't noticed him, though that seemed unlikely since he'd made a point of being obvious. As his blood pounded and he compelled rhythmic breathing to try to maintain a clear head, Grey didn't quite know what to do.

Finally — after two or three whole seconds — Pierce noticed that the Lord she was shadowing was ready for a fight. Coming forward out of the shade and drawing her own pistol from her waistband, she hurried forward to a point a dozen yards to his left, but in line with him. It was important to maintain good spacing, in case someone opened fire on them.

But Pierce didn't see the reason for Grey's concern, and as she assumed her own shooting crouch, she glanced at her senior fellow, "Where?"

Grey looked away from the cape just long enough to nod in its direction, "There."

Then he looked back, and it was gone.

A crucial mistake, and Grey's eyes widened as he realized what he'd done. As he'd been trained by Smith to do, the young Lord quickly let his gaze traverse the campus in front of him. He looked from left to right and back again, trying to see if he could spot his missing adversary.

But she wasn't in sight.

"Damn," was all he managed to say quietly to himself, then waved his hand low at Pierce.

"She disappeared, we must find her."

Though she'd not seen any danger herself, the talented Lady nodded in reply. There was no doubting Grey.

Together, then, the two Champions began a harried search. Never again did they see the cape.

CHAPTER X

With so many Lords and Ladies away on protection duties, the Champions Club in Jimmystown was quite empty when Alex and Stephanie burst through its front door later that afternoon.

"I was sure it was six," Stephanie was saying as the door shut behind them, but Alex shook her head.

"I only wanted five. We had to leave some for the rest of the base..."

Both girls' pockets were loaded with extra magazines for their Brownings, but considering the small size of Alex's pockets in particular, that wasn't so many. Still, they'd managed to leave the poor Sergeant on watch in a very disoriented state, and likely not realizing that he'd handed two of the newest troublemakers in the Special Service Regiment the capacity to shoot far more than was usually considered necessary by British Army regulations.

"We'll have to do a count," Stephanie concluded as they advanced through the front hall of the Club — a building that was much more like a large house than a social center. Both had been guests at parties here from time to time, so they knew their way around... but they were surprised by how quiet it was.

Alex finally stopped in the entranceway, craning her neck slightly and narrowing her eyes as she listened for sounds of activity, "There are only a few people here... guess everyone else is out guarding against Emily."

"Good, we won't be interrupted," Stephanie flashed a smile before nodding towards the nearby double doors that led to the common room.

Matching that bright expression, Alex followed her Second Lieutenant to the door, then pushed it open. She hadn't expected anyone to be inside — her hearing was supposed to have detected a big soldier slurping on some homemade chicken soup. Of course, it failed her this one time, so both she and Stephanie jolted to a stop at the sight of the fellow.

He wasn't just slurping soup, he was also reading a newspaper with no seeming awareness of the door having opened... but both girls could tell he knew they were there. Worse: it was almost as though he'd been waiting for them.

And based on the stripes on his arm, he was a Sergeant.

The math wasn't difficult.

For a full minute, Alex and Stephanie both stood in the door and stared at the intruder who'd somehow made it to their secret lair before they'd even thought to come to the place. In turn, the Sergeant continued to slurp his soup, apparently fascinated by the day's *Evening Telegram*.

Standoff.

The tension mounted quickly — silence always had that effect amongst people jockeying for position — and eventually, Alex and Stephanie cast glances at each other. Someone had to say something, but they didn't want to be first. To strike first was to concede defeat.

Bearing that in mind, Alex had an idea. With a nod in the direction of the Sergeant's table, she bounced her eyebrows and basically suggested to Stephanie that they sit down. Years of friendship enabled the smooth passage of that unspoken message, and the American Lieutenant replied with a silent nod.

Carefully — comically — the two girls then proceeded to tip-toe into the common room, basically trying to sneak up on the man who clearly knew they were there. For his part, the Sergeant played along, continuing with his delicious soup and his engaging paper.

Complete silence endured. No hands were going to be tipped while the Lady and her Lieutenant were still standing, so with a shrug, Stephanie pulled out one of the chairs opposite the Sergeant and planted herself in it slowly — almost as if she thought it might break under her. Of course it didn't, and as she let out the breath she'd been holding, she looked up to Alex with a second shrug. That was prompting enough: Alex sat down too.

For a moment, they both stared at the Sergeant, but he continued to study his paper. A very cool customer, this fellow — and his face was entirely neutral. Neither stern nor amused, he just seemed to be reading while two young women awkwardly menaced him.

Alex decided to go even further: shimmying in her seat, she pushed the tails of her coat aside and started tugging the magazines she'd acquired out of her pockets. Thinking that to be a fine idea, Stephanie did the same.

The Browning mags were soon lined up on the table in front of them like dominoes. Between them they'd acquired fourteen, which was clearly too many, but neither of them wanted to say that aloud. Instead, they shared another look that expressed the awkwardness of the situation, then drew their pistols, made sure they were empty, and laid them on the table as well.

And the Sergeant kept reading. Though, Alex realized, he'd been on the same page for quite a while — perhaps he was just staring at that page as though he was reading.

Glancing again to Stephanie, she began to suggest as much with a brief nod of her head towards the paper...

"I see you found your girls, Colour Strong!"

Silence shattered like a pane of glass, but at least it was none of these three who'd broken it. Instead, Missus Reid, the woman who had run the Champions Club since its inception, swept into the room with a tray carrying cups of tea and a plate of lemon squares.

"Hello girls," she smiled warmly at her new arrivals, then came alongside the table and laid down her tray. "I brought these for the Colour, but you'll share, won't you, Mike?"

All of a sudden, Strong was animated and smiling, "Of course I will, Colleen. Your soup was lovely, by the way — I really do think you should bring some for the girls."

The crafty man had managed to speak about them without actually speaking to them. Clever. Alex wasn't about to let that go, so she looked up to Missus Reid with a shake of the head, "I was actually really craving some pan fried cod. Don't suppose that could be done up?"

"Of course it can!" was the answer — because there was never a dish that a Newfoundland kitchen wouldn't find a way to provide for a guest.

"Ooh, I'll have that too," Stephanie added with a grin, and Missus Reid nodded.

"Won't take long. Don't you have too many squares or you'll spoil your supper!"

With that the woman departed, closing the common room's doors behind her. The standoff resumed, with Strong immediately looking back to his paper. But this time he didn't have soup.

Stephanie and Alex traded one more glance, deciding they had to extend the olive branch. It was Alex who led, because Champions were supposed to do that: "Alright Sergeant, you can't possibly keep this going without soup as a prop."

"I could try," he answered, immediately dropping the *Telegram* and smiling across the table at his challengers. "But I think we've all proved our points."

Stephanie leaned forward and laced her hands in front of her on the table, "I don't know, I was still sort of proving mine."

"No, you were finished," Strong disagreed, his smile broadening. Then he waved one hand at the array of magazines in front of him. "I hope you left old Billy Binford alive at the armory."

Alex narrowed her eyes slightly, then countered, "A couple of harmless cheek-kisses. Something you'd know about, *Colour Strong*."

Grinning because he'd been recognized, Mike Strong held up his hand, "Guilty. And though I rarely limit my kisses to cheeks, I highly approve of you young ladies being so modest. Since I have to keep you out of trouble now."

So there it was: the gauntlet had been thrown down.

Stephanie went first: "You make a habit of kissing Sergeants in places other than the cheek, Colour?"

He didn't miss a beat: "I shared that in confidence. I expect you to tell not a soul, or I'll turn you both in for theft."

"That doesn't sound like much of a way to keep us out of trouble, though, does it?" Alex attacked from the flank, but Strong had simultaneously charmed enough ladies to know how to wheel on the defense.

"I never said I'd be any good at it," was his answer. "My specialty will be keeping you from falling pray to n'ere-do-well Lotharios. And also machine gun fire. But for all things, ladies, I have only one rule for you to remember. This one rule... and really, it's a question... will get you through any dire situation you care to name. And as such, I need you to hear it, and live it, immediately."

Alex frowned, recalling as much as she could about Mike Strong's reputation. Everyone knew something about the Sergeant who'd survived the new world, and punched the War Minister. Didn't he have a catchphrase?

"What... would Mark Strong do?" Stephanie was first to recall the words, and the Sergeant sat back with a satisfied smile.

"Of course my reputation precedes me. My name is actually Mike, but otherwise you're quite right, you wise young officer. I want you both to ask yourselves that question whenever you're in danger, be it from a lover boy or some savage bent on tearing you limb from limb. The answer will see you through alright."

Strong folded his arms, and Alex frowned slightly — but with an almost-smile at the same time: "Will it ever actually make sense? Colour, I'm going to be honest, you seem to be trying really hard to make a first impression..."

"Says the Lady who tiptoed in here and was desperate not to speak first because she thought she'd surrender the upper hand... and still spoke first anyway," he didn't pull his punches, and that plain truth drew a nod from the Lady.

"But that's fair enough," he went on. "We all know we're sizing each other up, but I'd appreciate it if you played along. I'm a sad old soldier with few pleasures in life."

"I'd heard you enjoy more than a *few* pleasures," Stephanie rallied, and Strong grinned.

"It's not always about quantity, sometimes it's quality."

"But nice to have both?" Alex surged again, and the Sergeant pointed to her.

"Oh yes, you've got that right," his smile got very big. "But back to my catchphrase: I want you to imagine this dangerous scenario. You are at a social function, the kind young ladies attend. A hop, maybe, because you two look like real Jitterbuggers. And I'm not there. Then a real ladies' man comes up to one of you... say you, Lieutenant. As soon as he starts talking, you ask yourself, what would Mike Strong do?"

Stephanie raised her eyebrow, "What would you do if a boy came up and started trying to seduce you, Colour?"

"Alas, only in my dreams... but play along: if the boy was charming, and clever, and manly, and painfully handsome, and capturing your heart with the quickest look..."

Alex's eyes narrowed again, "Wait, are you describing yourself?"

Strong paused and shifted his gaze back to the white-coated Lady, "I am *mostly* describing myself. But because I'm more modest than this brat trying to make eyes at you, I'm not mentioning all of my fine qualities."

"Thank God for your restraint, or we'd both be head over heels instantly," Stephanie was merciless with her retort, but Strong met her with another pointed finger.

"None of that, young lady. I know it will be difficult for you to resist, but this is serious military business and we'll have none of that. Ever. I know your parents."

"Of course," Stephanie nodded, making sure to look chastened for ever having entertained the fantasy.

Without pause, then, Strong returned to his example: "So, if you are confronted with a fellow who is, when it comes down to it, as close to manly perfection as he can be, without being me, I want you to take out one of these Brownings you have on the table here, and shoot him in the foot."

Alex hadn't been expecting the violent turn, so she was sure to look surprised, "Colour, I would never shoot you in the foot!"

He paused at that, and for a second Alex wondered if he didn't have an answer for her. But of course he did, "Yes, you do look like the type who'd aim *higher*. I'm just hoping your gunplay isn't as good as hers."

With that, he bobbed his head towards Stephanie, and the Lieutenant took the invitation to engage with Alex, "Don't worry, I'll shoot him for you."

She then stuck out her hand towards her friend, and with some silly sense of formality, the young Champion shook it, "Agreed."

And then she turned her hand towards the man across the table, leaning forward so he could reach it more easily,

"I'm Lady Alex Smith, Mike. Shake my hand so we can make this official."

He did shake her hand, with a grin, "Honored, M'Lady."

"Probably best not to call her that," Stephanie extended her hand as well, and as Strong shook it, he agreed.

"Whatever you say, *ma'am*."

They would definitely have to work on their choice of titles, but that would be for later; for now, Stephanie sat back as a silence descended over the table — not an awkward or even intentionally-strained silence, but a warm one. Smith had chosen the right NCO for this job, that much was clear.

"I knew you'd curse us," Alex eventually said to her friend, recalling the American's assertion that no Sergeant would be able to handle them.

The young officer tilted her head and then glanced sideways at Strong, "I'd promise not to make the same mistake next time, but I don't know how we're going to get rid of this one."

Strong leaned back in his chair, "Who says it won't be me trying to get rid of both of you?"

Alex and Stephanie looked at each other, and it was the Champion who answered with a shrug, "That happens to me a lot. I can't even convince a seagull to regurgitate dinner for me."

Stephanie winced — it really was the worst possible time to try to resuscitate that joke.

Strong didn't seem to notice, "Are we talking about a particular gull? Because I'll fistfight any bird who was behaving wrongly to my Champion. Might even win."

"I think he had kids. Was just looking for a girl on the side," Alex shook her head, then planted her elbow on the table and rested her chin sadly in the palm of her hand.

With a disgusted shake of the head, Strong made a promise: "Typical flyboy. If you see him again, just you point him out to me."

Alex nodded with all sorts of pretend earnestness, but even in the midst of the repartee she was studying the Colour. He was not quite what his reputation would have suggested.

"So, will you be playing along with all our jokes, or just the bad ones?" Stephanie raised that question before the gull joke could stagger on any longer, and Strong paused thoughtfully.

"I don't know..." he began, then trailed off as if he was expecting someone to finish his sentence for him. Alex and Stephanie weren't ready for that, so they both just stared. And the silence started to get awkward.

"I don't *know*..." Strong repeated more forcefully, and then nodded towards the opposite side of the table. It wasn't that hard to notice a cue, surely?

Alex and Stephanie looked at each other, because they certainly weren't catching on to what he wanted them to say... or ask... oh right, that.

"I *don't know...*" he tried for the third time, and with her chin still resting glumly in her hand, Alex offered the reply.

"What would Mike Strong do?"

"There it is!" Immediately the Colour's smile broadened again as he looked between the girls, "See, wasn't that fun?"

Stephanie and Alex glanced at each other again, their expressions answering the question.

Then the young Champion made a wise observation: "Sounds like we're all going to play along with each others' awkward jokes. This will be a safe space for bad humor."

That sounded fine to Strong, and he nodded.

But Stephanie disagreed: "I think my jokes are good."

Alex and Strong both turned on the Lieutenant with frowns, and then the girl in white had to give her friend the bad news, "They really aren't."

"I have noticed, just from our time here, that they are pretty terrible," the Sergeant added reluctantly. "But we can work on that. With enough practice, one day you could be as funny as me."

Stephanie folded her arms, "That's what I'm afraid of."

Alex lifted her chin and raised her hand slightly to vote with her friend, "I would also be afraid of that."

"That makes three of us," Strong answered with an easy grin, and then they fell silent again. These three were stuck together, but as Missus Reid came back with food, they all got the feeling that would work out just fine.

CHAPTER XI

Caralynne was on the telephone in the living room, though she was mainly silent as she listened to Jimmy's information from Toronto. Smith had only been able to overhear pieces of his wife's part of that conversation, but he figured he had an idea of what was happening: the Champions at the Saa School thought they'd seen Emily, or whoever was in the cape, but now were unable to locate her.

Reinforcements would be sent out before morning — not more Champions, since the Lords and Ladies were too scattered to be able to field a sizable force, but probably an assault company from the Special Service Regiment. Ordinary soldiers might not be able to meet a rogue Champion on level terms, but few knew better how to contain a warrior with savage-born powers than the men who guarded them on a daily basis.

All of that was a concern to Smith — the world was even less stable than it had been a couple of days before — but it wasn't his only preoccupation. While he waited for his wife to finish on the phone, he stood in the hallway between his house's bedrooms, and studied the white coat that was hanging on the outside of Alex's door.

It wasn't particularly late — just past 10:00 in the night (2200 hours in army terms) — but his daughter was out like a light, as was Stephanie. They'd both come home from their first day of Champion orientation hopping around with excitement, telling stories of everything they'd done, and about their impressive new Sergeant.

After supper had started to settle, though, they'd both begun to suffer from heavy eyelids, and soon enough they'd gone to bed for what Smith predicted would be a particularly long sleep.

Before bedding down, Alex had decided on the right place for her new coat: on a hanger suspended by a nail from the front of her bedroom door. Smith hadn't understood why she'd hung the coat on the outside of her door until Caralynne had made a good point, "You've seen the state of her room? It's a *white* coat."

Alex wasn't a particularly messy girl, but then again Smith probably wasn't a man to judge. He'd spent years of his life sleeping on the dirt and living with a horse… he never had white clothes, but the white handkerchiefs and rags he'd owned had never stayed clean for long. How his daughter would keep her coat pristine, the former-drifter didn't know, but whatever state it was in, he knew the white suited her.

Smith tested his thumb and forefinger by rubbing them together. Once he was satisfied there was no grit or dirt on either, he reached out and gently tugged on the sleeve of the bright garment, assessing its strength and softness. It felt sturdy, but wasn't coarse... a mix of qualities his daughter shared.

That made it a symbol of two things, he figured: a sign of the sort of woman she'd grown up into, and of the fact that she had indeed grown up. She wouldn't be around the house much anymore... she'd probably stay in her room whenever she was back in Jimmystown, but if she followed the path of most Champions who graduated, she, Stephanie and Strong would soon be assigned a section of infantry, and sent off to garrison a particular city for a year or two. There she'd become a local fixture and establish a life all her own.

Smith was sending his daughter off to the trail, a place he'd spent more than a decade before he found his way to settling down. It was an important time, and as he let go of Alex's coat, the former-drifter did feel some sadness.

But that was right — sending a daughter out into the world was supposed to make a man sad. Proud too, but sad for not having her nearby anymore. That feeling wouldn't change Smith's belief that Alex was free to go. It was her time, and he knew she was ready for it.

Figuring he'd thought as much on that subject as he needed to, the American turned away from his daughter's door and headed back to the living room. Caralynne caught his eye as he entered the warmly-lit space, holding up her hand to let him know she was almost done.

"That sounds good," she said immediately, making it sound as though she was wrapping up with Jimmy. "Alright. We can review the report again the morning... yes... right. Good night."

With that she hung up, then turned and let out a breath, "He's sending 'K' Company under Major Mitsui."

Smith approached her as she spoke, nodding as he digested the news, "Makes sense."

It was all he said before he lowered himself onto the couch beside his wife, while she pushed the phone back to its corner on the end table. The strain on her expression was clear enough as he put his arm around her shoulders, but instead of commenting on it he let her voice her concerns in her own time.

"So it could be Emily, which would be bad for a lot of reasons. But whoever it is... great timing that she shows up on this particular week," Caralynne said plainly, looking past Smith's face and down the hall to Alex's room.

Even in the dark, the white coat seemed to glow — perhaps not a great characteristic when it came to stealth.

"Better it happens while she's still close," Smith pointed out, and Caralynne's gaze shifted back to his face. He was right as usual — it would have been bad if Alex and Stephanie had been sent off to garrison a distant town... or worse, an important town... just when this dangerous Champion-killer was arriving on the scene. At least while she was in Jimmystown, she was under her mother's direct protection.

Taking a breath, Caralynne nodded very slowly, "Right again, husband."

Smith had been told by some men that being a husband meant he could never be right — that women held the exclusive reins on being correct, whether they were or weren't. That had never made sense to him, because he figured any marriage was a partnership in which both people could have the right idea sometimes, and maybe the wrong idea other times. The point was to make sure husband and wife helped each other be right more than wrong. Partners.

But then, Smith wasn't a common sort of man, and Caralynne certainly wasn't an ordinary woman. And perhaps because she'd once died within sight of her now-husband, she had no appetite to perceive any illusions to be true, whether they pertained to other people or herself. Everything about her life was a second chance — one she owed very much to Smith, who had come searching for her even when he'd known she was dead. She wasn't going to waste any of the time she had now.

And she certainly wasn't going to risk Alex. Especially if it *was* Emily out there, looking for some sort of twisted revenge.

"I'll keep them nearby for now..." she said eventually, then closed her eyes as she laid her cheek on Smith's shoulder. The American tightened his grip around her as she did that, and together they were silent for a time — because silence was all they usually needed.

Hopefully the assault company would find its target in Toronto, and Grey and his team could sort it out. There'd be more answers in the morning; until then, there was no point worrying.

It was later than Brigadier Kennedy had planned on staying out, but as he watched 'K' Company begin loading its rovers and equipment onto the skycruiser *George Tucker*, he knew the work at hand was vital.

Two hundred men, fifty trucks, and a whole load of guns were going to be in Toronto before sunrise, headed by Major Tokutaro Mitsui, an officer who'd joined the regiment on a learning exchange from Japan four years prior (and who Jimmy had refused to send back).

Kidnapping the best officers from all over the world was one of the Special Service Regiment's defining features; the use of assault companies was another. Rightly or wrongly, Kennedy and Jimmy had not organized their massive regiment like a British formation, but instead had built it out of units like the 'Commandos' formed by the Boers during their wars in South Africa. Lean and maneuverable, an assault company was meant to provide a Champion with much heavier support than any single lance ever could.

While there weren't any Lords or Ladies left in reserve at Jimmystown, the Fort had twenty such companies at any time, usually made up of men who'd previously been in lances and were waiting to serve again.

It was admittedly a haphazard structure, and Kennedy expected the continued growth of the regiment would soon warrant a reorganization, but for the moment it would get the job done. And whatever the administrative background, the Brigadier could think of few men better than Mitsui and 'K' Company to send to Toronto.

The loading process moved quickly and easily — one of the benefits of an elite regiment was that those who didn't meet its standards didn't last long, leaving it to the best soldiers to handle the tough work. All the men boarding *George Tucker* knew what they were in for, and despite being sent out at midnight, they didn't grumble. After they all got aboard, Mitsui drove his own rover up into the skycruiser's hold, then turned back towards the ramp just as it began to close.

Catching Kennedy's attention, the Japanese Major offered a sharp salute. The Brigadier returned the gesture, then the ramp finished rising and the big ship's massive engines roared to life.

Having seen skycruisers coming and going so much over recent years, Kennedy had no reason to brave the thrust of the machine just to watch it lift off; instead he turned away and headed back to his own rover. He'd driven himself up to Torbay Airport for its liftoff — his staff officer had a newborn at home, so disrupting his night just for a drive would have been unkind.

Now the Brigadier switched on his truck, fired up its headlights, and hurried off onto the darkened road that led from the airport — a narrow strip of twisting tarmac called Major's Path. Dense trees crowded in close on both sides, and a thin mist was limiting visibility, but Kennedy had driven the Path in the dark many times. It was not a concern. Though he didn't press his rover hard, the Brigadier was doing a good clip when he came around a corner... and was confronted by a figure in a cape.

"Jesus!" he cranked the wheel hard, and the rover's sophisticated suspension — benefiting in part from the reverse engineering of Hubrin lorries — was able to keep all four of its wheels on the tarmac as it weaved to avoid the obstacle.

Adrenaline surging into his veins, Kennedy slammed on the breaks as soon as he'd regained control, then he leaned back over his seat and collected a Thompson submachine gun from the arms box there. He was sure he'd seen... a cape...

Though he was a general officer now, Shawn Kennedy knew his way around a gun. It took only a few seconds for him to prime his weapon — fast enough, he hoped, if some rogue Champion was fixing to jump him. As soon as it was ready, he pulled a hand torch from the storage box beside his seat and hopped out of his rover.

There was just enough moonlight for the Brigadier to see basic shapes unaided; that in mind, he pocketed the torch and shouldered his Thompson as he moved carefully down the side of his vehicle.

The figure was still standing beside the trees two dozen yards behind, and as he got it in his sights, Kennedy felt the hairs on his neck standing at attention. It had been years since he'd felt such tension, but now old instincts came back and he called out: "Who goes there?"

There was no answer, and well aware that a Champion might cover the distance between them before he even got a shot off, Kennedy planted his feet, "I'm Brigadier Kennedy of the Champions Regiment. Identify yourself."

The shadowy night didn't provide much detail for Kennedy to work with when it came to identification; a large dark shape... two skinny-seeming legs sticking out of a bulbous silhouette... the sort of outline that was probably formed by a person in a cape putting his or her hands on his or her hips...

And suddenly the person moved.

But its legs bent the wrong way.

With a snort, the moose backed out of the woods it had been half-standing in, clearly still chewing on whatever it had been eating.

"Oh thank God," Kennedy released a breath and then lowered his Thompson. "Jesus. Buddy, you took, like, four years off my life."

The moose stared at the Brigadier, its face in shadow but the direction of its head clear enough because with every exhalation, plumes of steam were shooting out of its nose. And it was still chewing.

"Well I can see you feel guilty about it, and thanks for the apology," Kennedy shook his head, holding up his hand in a wave at the great creature. "Now get off the road before you kill someone."

The moose continued to stand and chew as Kennedy hopped back into his rover, laid his Thompson in the passenger seat, and drove off. The last thing the Brigadier needed at midnight was a scare like that... so it was just as well he didn't look in his rearview mirror before he rounded the next corner.

Apparently the moose didn't mind the presence of a caped figure behind him, but then moose were notoriously nonchalant around a threat. And to be fair, he was in no danger. He continued to chew before moving on.

CHAPTER XII

"Ladies, allow me to present the Series II Land Rover, courtesy of Britain's fine Rover Motor Company."

Mike Strong was showing off, and as the sun rose over Fort Waller's motor pool, both Alex and Stephanie folded their arms and donned rather disinterested expressions. This seemed only to spur the Sergeant's enthusiasm, and as he walked around the green truck they'd been assigned, he gestured to it as enthusiastically as if he were an automobile sales model.

"You can pretend to be bored all you like, but I know you're both secretly very interested. And since I spent two years looking after these things, I can tell you every little detail," he grinned, then came to a stop at the vehicle's front and leaned against its hood.

"I am awash with joy," Alex observed flatly.

"It's a jeep," Stephanie's reply was similarly deadpan, but her careless words instantly twisted Strong's expression into one of horror.

"You mind your tongue, Second Lieutenant Shylock," the Sergeant said, then patted the rover's fender with reassuring words. "There there, she didn't mean that."

Alex met that display with a frown, "It's a horse?"

Strong shook his head, then folded his arms, "No, it's a Land Rover. People get this wrong all the time. Jeeps were first. Willys created them down in the US, thanks to the technology we reverse-engineered from the Hubrin lorries we took from the new world. They created them and they *trademarked* them. Land Rover came along when the British Army decided they didn't want to order all their kit from American factories. They're very good, but different too."

It was actually a lecture on... trucks and trademarks? Stephanie looked down at her watch as the scolding bounced off her, then frowned, "It looks like a Jeep."

"They are *very* different. And if you keep mixing them up like that, trademark men from both firms will come here and sue us all," Strong warned.

Stephanie raised her eyebrow, "I'll risk it."

"How long were you stuck clerking in the motor pool?" was Alex's question, and Strong paused in thought.

"Too long?"

That sounded right, and Alex nodded before dropping her arms and advancing towards the rover. Whatever it was supposed to be called, it certainly was an impressive vehicle — designed to be able to carry its passengers just about anywhere. Every lance was assigned at least one such vehicle to give its ordinary soldiers the chance to keep up with a running Champion... and these trucks (be they Jeeps or Land Rovers) could do just that.

"I rode partway to the Saa prison camp in an old Leyland truck back in 1920," Strong said, coming off the hood and following Alex with his eyes. "These rovers are a hundred times better. If we hadn't been able to borrow from Hubrin machinery, we probably wouldn't have seen anything like them for decades. You'll be glad to have them around."

"I didn't say I wasn't glad," Stephanie followed Alex towards the truck, then laid a hand on its fender. "I just happen to be American, so it's a Je—"

"If you keep saying it, he's going to keep talking about it, instead of letting us drive around making trouble," the young Champion interrupted, and Stephanie paused with a glance to her friend.

"It's a truck," she said instead.

Strong smiled, "Aha, so we're all happy."

"Now you're getting ambitious," Stephanie narrowed her eyes, and the Sergeant chuckled and shook his head.

"Always, *ma'am*."

Stephanie shot him a glare at that word, which caused him to smile again, but instead of continuing their verbal sparring match, the Second Lieutenant began circling her assigned vehicle, "I'd probably be more use on a horse."

It was fair to say that a girl who'd been raised where and how Stephanie Shylock had been wouldn't be naturally inclined towards a mechanical, wheeled vehicle for rapid transport. Of course she knew the benefits of the Land

Rover, but when it came down to it, she trusted her riding abilities more than its steering wheel.

"It's definitely a different beast," Strong agreed with a rather more thoughtful nod. "But maybe you want to have a test run in this beauty, see what it can do."

Stephanie shrugged, "Well I didn't think we were just going to spend the day running circles *around* it…"

"Speak for yourself," Alex smiled, then craned her neck in a slightly-self-satisfied manner. "That's right, I said it."

"I noticed," Strong added. "That's one of those bad jokes we're supposed to support you through, right? Laugh until it's over?"

Alex shrugged, "Well I'm not going to *ask you* to laugh. But if that's what you feel moved to do, then don't hold back."

With a single laugh that was clearly forced, the Sergeant turned to Stephanie: "Let's drive."

"You do realize how much trouble she's going to cause?"

Lady Anne Devlin had to smile at her son's concern, and as she did she replied with a nod, "I have some idea."

"Really? Because it's a lot of trouble."

George Devlin and his mother were walking on one of the trails north of Fort Waller, enjoying the cool mid-morning breeze that came through the trees as the sun began its daily climb. Though they were supposed to be speaking of matters related to their hospitality work, and specifically to whatever might have been gleaned from Captain Todd, young George's preoccupation was tragically predictable: he was worried about the regiment's new Second Lieutenant.

Certainly, George had spoken to his father in support of Stephanie's desire to be a soldier... but now the reality of her appointment was settling in, and he wasn't entirely thrilled about the prospect.

"Smith approved their Sergeant... Mike Strong, he was with us in the Newfoundland Regiment during the Hubrin War."

"He's the lunatic who punched the Minister of War," George offered that more recent assessment, and Anne raised her eyebrow.

"For the right reasons. He's the best possible man to look out for Stephanie and Alex, and he'll keep up with their wit."

That was a strong endorsement, but it didn't take the edge off George's concern. Stephanie, Alex and Strong were presumably going to be sent off on some strange adventures, and the new Lieutenant was a headstrong American girl who was tougher than she looked but not as indestructible as she probably thought.

"You just need to let her on her way, George. She's not the sort to listen to anyone telling her not to have an adventure. In time she might want to come back here and settle down with a handsome young gentleman, but right now she's too enamored by the promise of adventure."

Anne's wise observations were rooted in her own experience. She once had chased two mysterious ladies for a position as a maid, and then had ventured with them to the new world, where she'd married a Lieutenant on little more than a whim. It had all been quite irresponsible, but had clearly turned out for the best. Stephanie's course would undoubtedly be similar.

But that was small comfort to Anne and Jimmy's endlessly responsible son, who had been raised without any romantic notions about soldiering, or adventure. There were several reasons he was not in the army, and his parents' honesty about the trials of military life was one of them.

"I just... I suppose," George shook his head as they walked, and with his hands thrust deep in the pockets of his suit jacket, he briefly reminded his mother of Sir Julian Byng.

Setting that thought aside, Anne smiled and offered a suggestion: "You might allow yourself to see that there are some other eligible young ladies vying for your attention. Some of whom aren't four years older than you."

That George was smitten with Stephanie was no secret, and Anne saw no harm in it. However, the son of the Viscount of the Grasslands was considered one of the most eligible bachelors in Newfoundland, and indeed, the Empire. Anne had received questions from as far away as India — prominent families seeking a gallant husband for younger daughters and the like.

George could have any lady he pleased, but he was never the sort of fellow to take advantage of such positioning. He'd come to appreciate the rugged girl from the new world, and he was piling all his loyal affections onto her.

Poor dear...

"That's the thing," he answered Anne's comment. "I'm younger than her by four years, and yet I'm *still* the more mature one. How can that be?"

His single-mindedness made Anne's smile grow, "You did hear the part about the other young ladies who would be interested in your affections?"

George Devlin stopped dead at that question from his mother, and the Viscountess of the Grasslands halted beside him, her smile remaining as she detected his quizzical brow.

"Obviously I heard that, mother. Really, could you just allow me to be heartsick for a while? I'll give up on her in my own time."

The lucid statement seemed almost a contradiction, and from her smile Anne developed an amused frown, "If you know you're going to give up, why not start now?"

"Because I'm smitten, obviously. And why should I be in a rush? Much easier to long for the girl of your dreams, than actually pick a wife."

There was a certain amount of wisdom in that declaration, which was no surprise to George's mother — he was both youthful and mature in ways that might make men twenty years older quite jealous. His precocious ability to recognize the intricacies of a situation had grown out of his childhood, and the many days he'd spent in Jimmy's office, watching the Viscount and other men like Alain Lapointe, now the Canadian Prime Minister, and Sir Julian Byng himself, sort out the future of the Champions.

It had been quite an educational environment, and the lessons learned had well-positioned George for the work he was now doing in Jimmystown. He was the only man she trusted as part of her hospitality department, and he handled some of the most sensitive aspects of that job.

But, of course, he was still just nineteen — a man by all standards, but young enough to be allowed to be smitten and heartsick if he wanted to be. And to be fair, if Anne had been asked to choose a wife for her son, Stephanie Shylock would have been on top of her list.

"So," the mother decided to accede to her son's wishes, "how much trouble is she going to get into?"

"The Gods of Olympus will personally come down here to file complaints. I swear she will make a pet of the Nemean Lion, and when Heracles comes to try to kill the poor fellow, she will break his nose."

George also had the penchants of a classicist, and as soon as those were manifested his mother usually lost track of the conversation. Anne could speak competently about the nuances of any situation in present world politics, but she'd never bothered with the Greeks.

Realizing she'd just lost the plot, George shook his head

and sighed, "That means a *lot* of trouble, mother."

"I figured that part," Anne nodded with an indulgent smile, then put her hand on her son's forearm. "But not to worry, Caralynne is hardly going to let Alex out of her sight, which means Stephanie too. It'll all work out."

A mother's reassurance always had a disarming quality, even when it was probably somewhat fictional. Deciding to simply let the subject drop — for a time — George took a deep breath, then shook his head and began walking again. Then he realized that he and his mother had made good progress indeed — they were half a mile up one of the trails on the large hill that stood north of Fort Waller.

As he looked around and got his bearings, Anne smiled, obviously recognizing how her son's preoccupation had led him into the unknown. Happened often.

Then she heard a twig snap. Looking back down the trail, she saw no signs of an approaching person, and there was no one ahead either. Thick trees crowded either side of the path, so lines of sight were somewhat obscured...

"Did you hear that?"

For all his preoccupations, George Devlin was still an experienced operator. Though he wasn't from the same frontier lineage as Stephanie or Alex, he'd been on his share of Newfoundland trails, and had been snuck up on by those two girls plenty of times.

Now he had a sinking feeling that history was repeating itself: "Is someone out there listening?"

He turned from his mother towards the trees as he asked that question, and for the first time Anne was slightly surprised by her son's words — she hadn't jumped to the same conclusion, that perhaps a mischievous young Champion had spotted them from the woods and was now eavesdropping on their conversation.

Indeed, if that was happening, she'd have been rather offended — perhaps fun and games to some, but hardly appropriate.

"I'm serious. If you're out there you better show yourself," George was letting frustration creep through into his voice, but still no response came.

Moving up beside her son again, Anne frowned, "You certain someone's out there?"

George was frowning deeply, beginning to wonder the same. It wouldn't have been like either Stephanie or Alex to remain hidden when called out. Certainly, their mischief wouldn't have been appreciated, but they were usually good about owning up to their silliness.

Perhaps it had been nothing...

A cluster of robins started out of the trees to the left, and George held himself very still as he observed their launch. Those birds had been happily in a tree, ignoring both him and his mother. Their flight could mean something else was lurking nearby, and if it wasn't one or two tormenting females of the human species...

"Moose... bear... coyote..." George muttered to himself

under his breath, then put his arm out between his mother and the nearby brush.

"Think it's an animal?" she asked quietly, and George nodded, then reached under his suit jacket and drew his revolver from its shoulder holster.

The compact Colt Detective Special — his chosen sidearm for hospitality work — wasn't a natural gun for bear defense, but it was better than a stick, and the noise might have a profound effect on an animal not expecting it. Still, he wasn't about to creep into dense underbrush to see what manner of beast was staring at him.

"Let's head back. I think my melancholy has led us into a predator's path, mother."

"Alright," Anne agreed, slightly concerned but quite proud of her son's clarity under possible threat. He was a fine young man, just like his father. Whether a youthful girl like Stephanie would ever appreciate that remained to be seen... but some woman would.

Together they backed down the trail, eventually turning and walking straight back to the safety of the Fort.

Or, relative safety.

CHAPTER XIII

The sun had passed its peak as the rover lunged up a rather daunting slope in the Newfoundland wilderness, its engine growling as its wheels gripped the dirt and rocks to pull it forward.

This trail took them up at a ridiculously steep angle — one Stephanie wouldn't have tried with a horse — and as her insides seemed to pitch and yaw with the rapid changes in relative gravitational direction, she couldn't help but giggle.

"I know, right?" Strong was behind the wheel, giving the rover the gas and grinning ear to ear. Having campaigned in the ancestor of this very truck, the Sergeant was entirely delighted with the rover's abilities — it was almost (though not quite) as powerful as a Hubrin silver lorry. But unlike those alien rollers, it had the benefit of running on petrol, and having been designed with humans in mind.

With two seats up front and an open back featuring facing benches along each side, the truck could easily carry a half-dozen people and equipment... more in a pinch. It was tough as a box of hammers, had fine range, and excellent speed. Everything about it had been developed to be practical — it even had a canvas top that could be put up against the rain. Not that shelter was needed today.

It was, in short, perfect.

Determined to gain another endorsement of that fact, the Colour glanced back over his shoulder, "Isn't it lovely?"

In the back, Alex wasn't quite ready to employ that last word. Eyes wide and a death grip on the railings behind Stephanie's seat, she'd managed to plant her feet against the struts that secured the rear benches to the frame. She wasn't planning to release any point of secure contact until the rover finished fighting its way up the steep slope.

"This is *insane*," was her obvious reply, and Stephanie glanced back at the words, then laughed outright.

"It's amazing!"

Alex's eyebrows somehow managed to climb even higher up her forehead, "It could flip, and then I'd have to catch it. And then my coat would be a mess."

As she said it, she realized it might not have sounded the most well-reasoned argument against the rover's mad dash, but she was committed. Fortunately, Stephanie was enjoying the strange feeling of having her insides pulled every which way far too much to offer a counter; she simply shook her head and looked forward at the sky that was growing between the trees as they climbed.

The engine was growling low but steady — the rover wasn't climbing on anger, but on pure, consistent strength. It was more than a little impressive, and the American

Lieutenant giggled again — something that was rare for her.

"Well," she declared after another moment, "I'm having fun!"

"You would..." Alex could only shake her head, and Strong just kept focused on the trail.

It was actually fair to say he was showing off — this particular hill was one of the most formidable climbs on the testing ground used by the motor pool to train men on their vehicles, and if the weather was wrong, back-sliding down the slope was entirely possible.

Worse things could happen too.

But the day was dry, and he was in fine form showing off the rover to his two new charges. Just a little bit further to the top now — as long as the engine didn't quit, or something didn't force them to stop, they'd be alright. Momentum was important on a slope.

"Um, moose?"

Strong blinked because he saw it too: a moose had wandered out onto the trail ahead of the rover, right at the crest of the hill. It was a big feller with quite a set of antlers, and as he sauntered out at the top of the steep trail, he paused and looked down. Obviously he wasn't sure what to make of the rover that was crawling towards him...

So he decided to just stand and watch.

"I didn't think they liked steep slopes," Stephanie looked immediately to Strong, and the Sergeant shook his head.

"He's at the top, it flattens out..." he replied, then looked back over his shoulder. "M'Lady, can you fish out a Garand from the arms box and give him a shot?"

Alex was staring up at the moose as well, but as she heard that request, she frowned, "What?"

Strong's tone had shed its earlier humor; he didn't want to try to stop on the trail, because he knew how dangerous the descent could be if the rover lost its grip. But the track wasn't wide enough to go around the great big moose, and if they tried to hit him — particularly at this angle — machine and animal would be tumbling to the bottom in a big wreck.

"We need to get him out of the way, Alex," Stephanie clarified, her own tone going serious as well.

"Obviously, but you want to shoot the poor fellow and have him fall down on us?" was the Champion's point, and she shook her head. "I'll deal with this."

Without pause, she adjusted her grip and repositioned her feet. Then, when Stephanie looked back to tell her friend just to get the gun, she discovered the back of the truck was empty.

"Uhm," she said, and Strong glanced at her.

"What?"

The moose was not expecting a person-sized bird of prey to land beside his shoulder, but true to his nature, he simply stood there and watched as Alex completed her majestic leap and landed on the steep trail without so much as a bobble. Looking back down towards the rover, she gauged time and distance, then concluded she had half a minute to encourage the moose to depart.

"You wouldn't mind moving, would you? There's a good fellow…" she tried, but the moose just stared at her. "Guess not. You haven't heard anything about me from a gull, have you? Because he'd be lying."

Shockingly, that didn't work either. Still, the joke's failure did leave her other options: she had her Browning, so she could fire into the air to try to scare the big fellow away. She could also try to make a moose call, to either distract or confuse him sufficiently to make him walk on. Or she could try something less elaborate.

"Fine. Just remember I asked politely first," she said, and then she reached out and shoved him.

By all appearances, this was a largely placid moose — not nearly so aggressive as some of the big brutes found around Newfoundland — but no one likes to be pushed. Unfortunately, he wasn't just pushed, but shoved by a Champion of the British Empire. He staggered sideways, then backed up a few steps as Alex put her hands on her hips and glared at him.

"Go on, before someone shoots you."

The moose faced Alex as he backed off, then his head dropped low and his eyes got a bit more intent. Observing the body language for a moment, the young Champion decided he was seriously considering a charge — which she supposed she deserved.

But if he charged right at the crest just as the rover was coming up... well.

Quickly crouching, young Lady Smith launched herself skyward again, passing over the moose from above and then landing behind him. He swung his head around, apparently reading her move pretty well, but remained still as she landed a few yards behind him. He didn't shift his feet, and for a second she wondered whether he'd just move off...

How he mistook her for another bull moose, Alex wasn't entirely sure, but he certainly seemed to. Head down, he pointed his impressive antlers right at her and leapt forward. It wasn't the attack of a predator — not like a wolf or a bear lunging for the kill — but anyone who discounted the immense power of a charging moose was asking for trouble. All he'd need to do was knock her over, then start trampling with his sharp hooves. That would be bad — especially for her coat.

Skipping back a couple of steps, Alex opened the distance faster than he could close it — even weighing more than 1,000 pounds he was fast, but he wasn't a Champion. Then she glanced very quickly around at the nearby terrain, and made her decision. Not certain whether a moose was likely to hold a grudge long enough to chase her (and the rover) for the rest of the day, she decided to discourage him.

Letting him get into range, Alex kept her eyes on his massive antlers. Then, as soon as they were near enough, she caught two of the smoother-looking edges with her hands, and pushed back.

The moose stopped dead in his tracks.

It was not easy — 1,000 pounds of wild Newfoundland moose was trying to win a pushing match, and he'd undoubtedly done this many times against his own kind. But as Alex's boots dug hard into the dirt of the trail, and her muscles awoke to the urgent duty they faced, he found himself facing a human with strength that simply didn't seem natural for her size.

He didn't give up, though; bull moose were accustomed to persisting when it came to pushing each other around, and even if this human had somehow stopped the first shove, she wouldn't be able to hold him when he really started driving...

Alex felt the moose's big push building up, and she clenched her jaw and crouched down to further lower her center of gravity... then she leaned into the moose before he was able to lean into her. His feet started to slip out from under him, so he took a few steps back, then a few more. But because of their relative positions, Alex realized she was pushing him towards the rover. They had to go a different direction, so she started side-stepping as she advanced. The big fellow had no choice but to follow — she had him by the antlers.

Once he was moving sideways, there was no way for the moose to really push back — he'd have to withdraw and reset — but he could panic plenty. His legs started lancing out in different directions, mainly trying to keep him upright, but also presenting a considerable danger to Alex — if he did manage to kick her, things could unravel. She needed him to stop panicking, so she began to push down.

There was no way for him to resist now: Alex made his nose touch the trail, and then shifted her grip and straightened out his head so that his whole chin could lie on the dirt. After that, she very carefully torqued his antlers so that his legs went out from under him, and he fell over.

With him completely down on his side, Alex crouched and continued to apply enough force to keep him planted. He struggled against her at first, but eventually he stopped trying — maybe giving up, or perhaps realizing she didn't intend him any particular harm.

"Deep breaths," Alex advised the poor fellow, and his heavy snorts suggested he was probably following her advice, whether he understood it or not.

In that precarious position, they both watched the rover crest the slope, and roll to a stop once it hit relatively level ground. Stephanie stood up in her seat immediately, a Garand rifle in hand and its strap wrapped around her arm to help with stability.

"No need for that," Alex called to her friend. "He's had a bad enough day without being shot."

That seemed obvious enough, though the young Second Lieutenant's natural instinct was different: "But, supper?"

"We're eating at the Ivory Wharf tonight," Alex shook her head as she called back, and then she looked down at the bull, who was gazing back up at her. "Hear that? We're not shooting you."

He snorted again, which she decided to take as a good sign, and then she looked back up to the rover. By now Strong was standing in his seat as well, and along with Stephanie he was watching the display with open-mouthed surprise.

Satisfied that the moose was sufficiently placid after his defeat, and that his natural instincts after being bested would see him run away, Alex slowly reduced the pressure that was holding his head to the ground. Feeling the change in force, he began to raise his head, and Alex let him up slowly, keeping her hands on his antlers the whole way.

Even with his head held low by Alex's grip, he towered over her — something the Champion herself was less aware of, but which was decidedly obvious to Strong and Stephanie. This giant moose stood still as she held onto him... and then she withdrew one hand... and the other hand.

His head slowly came up, and wondering whether he'd take his chance to swing at Alex, Stephanie shouldered her Garand and took aim. She wasn't exactly eager to have to drag back a 1,000-pound bull moose, or clean it, but if he made a move...

"Go on," Alex nodded her head in the direction of the

woods beside the trail, and the moose snorted at her before walking off.

Stephanie let her rifle drop from her shoulder and called out to her friend, "Did you just wrestle a moose?"

As that question was asked, Alex turned back towards the rover, dusting each hand against the other with a frown, "Is my coat still clean? I think I need to wash my hands..."

Stephanie looked from her friend to her Sergeant, and found Strong's own face was a picture of surprise. Of course he'd been marching with Champions since 1919, and knew what they could do, but it was rather rare to see one demonstrating power so overtly as Alex had just done. Pinning a *bull moose*, literally with her *bare hands*?

"Wrestled a moose without so much as a spot on her coat," Strong shook his head with some absurd reverence. "The legend begins."

Alex hopped into the back of the rover as he spoke, and her response was predictable, "So my coat's clean?"

"The legend of whitecoat," Stephanie picked up on her Sergeant's needling, and sat down in her seat with a shake of the head. "There'll be no living with her now."

"And that means my coat is clean?" Alex was fixated, and with a grin, Stephanie looked back.

"Yes, it's clean. But when it comes to the legend, we'll leave out the part where you keep asking about it. It's not very heroic."

Alex considered her friend disapprovingly, "I'm sorry,

I didn't hear you over the sound of how white my coat is. Colour Strong, are we just planning to sit here, or perhaps can we move on?"

"On our way, M'Legend," he rather cleverly modified her title, and Stephanie pointed that out to him with a smile.

"I see what you did there… changed her title…"

"It was good, wasn't it?" Strong replied, and Stephanie nodded with great enthusiasm.

"Amazing!"

Alex rolled her eyes and moved to cup her forehead with her hand… but stopped when she realized her palm did smell a bit funny after the wrestling match. She decided not to touch her face (or her coat) until she found soap and water.

She didn't mention that, though, because she figured it might have ended up in the legend of whitecoat.

CHAPTER XIV

Lord Jimmy Devlin preferred the days when he was able to get out of the office. It had been more than a decade since the Viscount of the Grasslands had properly taken men into the field, and he still missed the feeling. With new dangers becoming apparent, and the future work of the regiment growing more dangerous, the men deserved the attention of their leader, and that was not something he could provide while sitting behind his desk.

So on the afternoon Alex was unintentionally building her legend, Jimmy had made a point of joining Captain Hans Ghale in training exercises with 'C' Company, another assault formation that was constantly ready in case circumstances warranted its heavy intervention. With 'K' Company gone to join Grey in Toronto, 'C' would be next up if a call came in.

Or, to put it less coyly, if a rogue Champion appeared somewhere, and men were needed to capture her.

Unsurprisingly, the afternoon's exercises had gone well. The men of the Special Service Regiment were the very best in the Empire: sharp as the Guards, tough as the Gurkhas (of which Ghale was one), and smarter than Jimmy himself

— though that last bar was rather low. They volunteered from all over the world, making them a variety of shapes, sizes and colors, and once they made it through selection, there was no question of them being anything but elite.

While the crotchety British MP Winston Churchill might call them 'Commandos', the Viscount simply called them the 'b'ys', because though they weren't all born in Newfoundland, they had all been adopted by this place, much as Smith had once been. And as a part of that tradition, these Special Service men had continued the Royal Newfoundland Regiment's love of vicious humor and irreverence, especially when it came to their superior officers.

That was a complicated way of saying they made merciless fun of Jimmy.

By the time the afternoon's exercises were done, the Viscount was surprised he had any skin left at all... but the day had been highly worthwhile. Whatever was going on in the world, and whoever was really after the Snapdragon plans, men like those of 'C' Company were a damned fine force. Soldiering with them, even just for half a day, left him with a feeling of some confidence.

Unfortunately, it also left him with a backlog of paperwork. He probably should have spent his afternoon at his desk.

It was getting into late evening by the time Lord Jimmy wandered in through the front door of his oversized

Headquarters, pulled his beret from his head and said hello to the clerk at the entry counter. Hurrying up the stairs to the second floor, he nodded to various officers and men as he passed them, then turned down the corridor leading to his own wing. This was a ridiculous waste of space: a long, wide, tall hallway that led solely to his office. Jimmy got the feeling that the designers wanted Gregorian chants to sound whenever someone passed through, but unfortunately for them, the Viscount didn't think so much of his own importance.

Indeed, the decoration was the only thing that made this corridor the slightest bit tolerable: at Jimmy's insistence, the walls were covered with photos and paintings of his fallen friends from the Royal Newfoundland Regiment. Every time he — or anyone — made the pilgrimage to his office, it was important that these fallen b'ys were remembered.

But that was all very somber, and given his more upbeat mood, Devlin left such thoughts behind, replacing them with a healthy anxiety about the number of papers that would be sitting on his desk. Jimmy's chief of staff loved torturing him with that sort of thing.

As he emerged into his outer office, Jimmy half-hoped that Lieutenant Parsons, his taskmaster, would be gone home for the evening. But of course he wasn't; sitting behind his desk as Jimmy arrived, the young officer didn't even look up as he offered his greeting: "Papers are on your desk to sign."

Stopping with a grimace, Jimmy considered a complaint, but knew it wouldn't help his case. Parsons was twenty years younger and many ranks lower, but there was no question that he ran the administrative side of the Special Service Regiment. Instead of whining, then, the Viscount tried to sound enthusiastic. He failed, "Anything else, or is that my only labor for the evening?"

Parsons still didn't look up: "The Prime Minister of Canada called, told me there are no developments in Toronto. Asked me to tell you that he's jealous you were recapturing your youth for an afternoon. Next time he visits he wants to be allowed the same."

That actually did make Jimmy smile, "Phone Alain back and tell him he can visit any time. Anything else?"

"The Prime Minister of Newfoundland says you're juvenile and that you shouldn't be out of your office at a critical time like this," Parsons' tone didn't change at all, and Jimmy actually laughed.

"Call him back and tell him to go to hell."

"I told him that would be your answer," the Lieutenant confirmed. "Now go sign your papers."

There was no more delaying to be done; Jimmy tried giving Parsons a withering glare, but the young man still didn't look up from his reading, so it was a waste. Collecting himself, the Viscount therefore opened the door to his office and stepped inside, ready to confront his fate.

As he paused for some procrastination, he looked over

his office. It was much too big. Alain Lapointe had once suggested that it could have held a small dance, were the furniture pushed to the sides. On the wall to the right were even big doors leading out onto a grand balcony, perfect for a musical interlude like in a Fred Astaire picture. Lovely.

At least those doors were open now, letting a breeze into the cavern. That was a help... unless it became a distraction.

But there was no point waiting any longer: advancing towards his desk, Jimmy started to consider the piles of paper that awaited him. They didn't look so big from across the room, but as he got closer, they started to grow fast. His whole evening might be taken up if he let it... maybe he could be like Caralynne, and jump off the balcony to escape Parsons' slave driving.

"I suppose you've gotten used to the paperwork?"

Jimmy Devlin managed to take one step after that question came from behind him, but then he stopped in place — froze, in fact.

"The trials of being a great Viscount of the Empire. Congratulations on the move up from Baron, by the way. I saw it on the news and considered sending a note, but it probably wouldn't have been appropriate."

It was strange to hear a voice for the first time in more than a decade... and to recognize that voice immediately. Jimmy's heart rate climbed as recognition set in, and he tried his best to gauge how far behind him the speaker was — how much time she might permit him to draw his Webley revolver from its holster, and turn, and aim...

Not enough time, of course. Because however big his office was, it was a mere sandbox to anyone who could move with the speed of a Champion.

Let alone for the first Champion herself.

"I suppose you knew it was me in New York. And you figured out what I was there for, didn't you Jimmy? So you sent all your spare Champions away to Toronto and to London, and kept how many here, exactly? Just the students at the Academy, and their teachers? The ones who weren't fit for action. Well, right now you'll be realizing that wasn't wise, won't you?"

There weren't too many options for Jimmy in this moment — he was armed, but he wasn't nearly fast enough to take advantage of that fact. Parsons was just outside the door, but he'd be no more help. And of course his guest was correct: aside from the small class of students and their teachers, the only Champion in the Fort or the adjoining Academy was Caralynne.

Wherever she was...

So with nothing to do but talk, Jimmy took a breath and slowly turned, "Hoped I'd get away with it. Never really thought you'd come back here."

By the time he finished saying it, he'd rotated suffi-ciently to see a woman in a dark cloak, wearing round tinted glasses, standing a dozen yards behind him. Because of the size of his office, that also put her a dozen yards from the door, with her back to it. She was smiling at him, but the expression was more sinister than anything else.

"I have, Jimmy," she said.

"That's quite obvious," he answered, then added her name: "Emily."

He fell silent for a moment after that, and studied the Lady who he had once done so much to protect. In the broadest physical terms, she seemed quite like her old self... a little more seasoned and filled out, but essentially the same woman.

The air about her was different, though — and given his suspicions, that was hardly a surprise.

"So," Jimmy said as he stared at her. "You're here for what purpose? Am I important enough to warrant being assassinated, or is this just a courtesy visit to taunt me?"

Tilting her head and folding her arms, the Lady considered him almost as though he were insignificant, "I haven't decided yet. But what I do need is the information in your Saa screen. Whatever data you wouldn't like to provide me about your Saa- and Hubrin-based technologies."

Jimmy raised an eyebrow, "Right, you're after our latest kit. You want Snapdragon."

"Do you have it?" the Lady's question was cool, and Jimmy took the chance to fold his arms, then shake his head.

"Do I look like I've taken up aeronautical engineering since you disappeared? I have a lot of things in that screen, but not Snapdragon."

The Lady smiled, "I'll take what you have, then. All of it. And you know better than to resist me."

At this point Jimmy knew he could object — could point out that he was the only one with all the passwords to access to the information his intruder sought. If she killed him, she'd get nothing, and he could have smugly said as much.

But if he did that she'd undoubtedly leave his office and seek out someone like Annie, then threaten her... or worse, actually harm her. It would be a great deal of theater and grief, for which the Viscount of the Grasslands had no appetite.

"Have a seat while I access the system?" he asked, turning back towards his desk and the massive Saa-built moving picture screen beside it.

"I prefer to stand," she replied.

Caralynne wandered into the Jimmy's outer office and nodded to Parsons, "He in yet?"

"Just got back," the Lieutenant replied. "Think he's contemplating a jump off the balcony to avoid doing his paperwork."

"Sounds like him," Caralynne smiled.

Moving towards the door, the principal of the Academy took a breath. She'd spoken to Alex after their rover had made its way back into the Fort, and it sounded as though Colour Strong was working out. There was also some whitecoat legend about to start, though the details remained unclear.

Certainly there were elements of the sublime involved, but on the whole it was good news that she knew Jimmy would like to hear.

Caralynne stopped halfway to the door and cocked her head slightly; Jimmy was speaking to someone inside his office. Parsons would have mentioned if someone was supposed to be in with him... but because of the heavy construction of the walls in the Headquarters building, the young adjutant likely couldn't hear the voices — he lacked Caralynne's Champion hearing. But there was definitely a conversation happening.

Then Caralynne heard a woman's voice — a voice that hadn't changed much, and yet sounded completely different.

Her mind abruptly cleared of all pleasant thoughts; she could feel her blood begin to pound more forcefully through her body at the presence of real danger. They had sent most of the Champions away, and kept only instructors in reserve. While Caralynne thought very well of the young Lords and Ladies who had elected to stay and teach the latest, smaller Academy classes, she knew none of them were particularly combat-ready.

And the voice she was hearing belonged to a woman who had been fighting with savage strength for decades.

This was beyond a problem.

Turning from the door, Caralynne moved silently over

to Parsons' desk, then reached down and picked up a pad of paper that had been in front of him. Looking up in surprise, the Lieutenant opened his mouth to question, but stopped when Caralynne put a finger to her lips. She then borrowed a pencil from him and wrote a fast note:

Hear EMILY inside. She can hear us. Walk downstairs, call out the regiment QUIETLY.

Parsons read the message with wide eyes, then nodded and quickly got to his feet, drawing a Browning from his desk drawer before hurrying silently away.

Turning back to the door, Caralynne took a silent breath. It was Emily — she was in Jimmy's office. And if she intended to make trouble, there was only one person who had the strength to stop her.

Pushing aside the tail of her brown jacket, Caralynne drew her Colt 1911 and moved towards the door.

"Awfully civil of you, just doing as I say. I must say I'm glad that you're as intelligent as I remember, Jimmy."

As he strummed away at the typewriter-like board that controlled his moving picture screen, Jimmy shrugged in response to his guest's praise, "Well I know how this would play out if I argued: you'd go find someone, threaten them, and I'd be forced to either sacrifice them or oblige you. Just seems better this way. It's not as though some blueprints or engineering specifications will be much good to you anyway. You can't do anything with them."

With that last comment, he glanced back across his office at Emily, and she smiled, "Oh Jimmy, I suppose you had to try. But no, I won't tell you what I'm doing, or if I'm working for someone, or if I have a whole team of the greatest engineers outside the Empire just waiting for plans so they can build an armada. Perhaps I'm just doing all this for sport."

"That'd be disappointing," the Viscount said.

"Very."

That last word came from neither Jimmy nor Emily. The sound of a pistol's hammer clicking back also didn't originate with either of them.

Emily let her chin dip when she heard it, then turned slightly and looked back over her shoulder, "As family reunions go, this one seems terribly tense."

Caralynne was standing in the open door to Jimmy's office, her Colt squarely aimed at Emily's back. She knew that gave her a slight advantage — she was charged and ready to shoot, while her sister of years past would have to produce her own pistol and turn before being able to respond.

But in such a relatively confined space as this office, that advantage was *very* slight.

"Emily..." Caralynne started to offer a reply, but found no words were adequate.

The resulting silence seemed to please the woman in the cape, "Has time made you speechless? I have rather missed your lectures, all these years. But I've taken them to heart, become truly responsible and have started thinking of others, not just myself. I promise."

Her tone was snide, even petulant — all the terrible things it had been in her worst private moments since 1920... since she'd lost Tom Waller, and had increasingly lost her notoriety.

That the tone still grated on Caralynne after a decade apart was instantly telling, but getting into a verbal sparring match now would serve nothing, "I hardly think this is the way we should start having arguments again."

Emily turned halfway around at those words, blading her body in Caralynne's direction and clearly clutching her own sidearm beneath her cloak, "You'd rather we just have a showdown, shoot to kill? Waste two more Champions in the service of ordinary people who don't deserve our loyalty?"

Caralynne's grip tightened on her Colt at the question, but she decided to counter with words instead of action, "You're going to try to have a philosophical discussion over gunsights?"

"I just want it clear that I didn't kill the boy in New York. That was his Sergeant, being a fool. Doing what they do..." Emily answered darkly, and it sounded very much as though she was reciting a piece of dogma that she'd come to believe... but which, lacking context, made very little sense to either Jimmy or Caralynne.

"The situation you created put Mister Steele in harm's

way," the Viscount made that point rather fearlessly from the other end of the room, and as Emily and Caralynne both looked to him, Jimmy had turned away from the Saa screen and rolled his chair closer to his desk.

Emily's glare fixed on him, "Out of respect for our past, I won't kill you, Jimmy. But you know better than most how your Champions are still viewed — still treated. Savages with clothes, that's all they'll ever be... their lives have little more meaning now than when you used to butcher them on the new world."

It definitely sounded to Caralynne as though this was a sermon she'd walked in on halfway — that Emily was fueled by some sort of anger that she believed was righteous, but was disconnected from reality.

"Why don't you come quietly, and then we can have a chat about this?" she suggested, and the woman in the cape shook her head, turning her eyes back to her once-sister.

"Be one with the family again?" Emily's words dripped with bitterness. "I won't kill you, Caralynne. But you will never be the same if you try to stop me."

"I'm just trying to figure out what the *hell* you're on about," was Caralynne's sharp riposte, and as she said it she tightened her grip on her pistol just a little more. She was very familiar with the trigger of her Colt — knew exactly how much pressure she could apply before it broke a shot. And she was getting close.

But if shooting began, Emily would move fast and

probably try to draw Caralynne's aim in Jimmy's direction, thus forcing her to hold her fire to avoid an accident. That would give the rogue Lady a brief advantage.

"I'm not here to cry and lament the ills of the world. I have my own plans, and you will thank me when they're done," Emily persisted, and Caralynne opened her mouth to respond... but Jimmy beat her to it.

"No need to lament," he said, and then he punctuated his words with the very distinct sound of a magazine locking into a Thompson submachine gun. "Surrendering wouldn't be a bad idea, though."

Emily's head whipped back around to face the Viscount, and as she saw he was hefting a submachine gun to his shoulder, she had to ask: "You keep a Thompson under your desk? What is this, Chicago?"

"I hate long meetings," was Jimmy's charming answer. "And while I'm pretty sure I won't hit you, I'll still let the whole damned Fort know you're in here. You really want to go up against thousands of men, all better armed and better shots than me?"

The calculus of the standoff changed instantly, and Caralynne fixed her gaze on Emily, watching a very slight shift in the caped-woman's posture as the gravity of the situation sunk in. The first Champion was powerful, but not immune to bullets — indeed, some of her problems on the new world had begun the day she was shot by a drunk while attempting to protect Tom Waller's sister.

That lesson still stood. Any firefight within the office would undoubtedly be a disaster for everyone involved — it was possible Jimmy and Caralynne could accidentally gun each other down, and the risk to Emily was nearly as great. And even a non-mortal wound could be devastating, because if she was injured and unable to take full advantage of her abilities, the ordinary men of the Special Service Regiment might indeed be able to capture her.

So it was time for discretion.

"This has been wonderful," Emily looked from left to right with those words. "We'll do it again soon."

Caralynne and Jimmy met eyes across the office, knowing she was about to flee and realizing the risks of trying to gun her down before she did far exceeded the benefits. Instead of shooting, then, both the Viscount and the Lady started towards the middle of the room, and by the time their feet began to move, Emily had blurred out the balcony doors.

"You keep a Thompson in your desk?" Caralynne asked as they arrived beside each other.

Jimmy shrugged and looked out the balcony doors into the late evening sky, "Long meetings, like I said. You warned Parsons?"

In answer to his question, a Thompson fired outside... and then a Garand. Some men had been ready for Emily. Looking to each other again, Caralynne and Jimmy hurried out through the doors, then leaned over the balcony railing.

Two men in battle dress were down on the ground, one clearly dead and the other with both legs bent in unnatural directions. Their weapons lay in the dirt beside them…

And Emily was gone.

"She'll probably be trying to get off the island…" Caralynne began a quick analysis, holstering her Colt as she spoke.

Jimmy kept his Thompson in hand, but nodded, "She was after data from the Saa screen… she might go after the skycruisers. Or the hospitality warehouse."

"I'll get the instructors up and armed to watch here and the warehouse, then go to Torbay…" Caralynne agreed, then started climbing up onto the balcony railing so she could leap down.

"I'll have Gallway deploy the whole Newfoundland Regiment to the airport, and get the assault companies ready to support wherever. Shame we don't have more Champions handy…" Jimmy replied. Then he halted, because there was one more Champion — one so new he'd overlooked her: "Where's your daughter?"

Caralynne blinked. Of course her daughter wasn't safe at home any more… now she wore a coat, and that meant she was supposed to help hunt Emily across the island of Newfoundland. Easily the most dangerous situation since… since the Hubrin battles on the new world.

Great first week for Alex.

Every maternal instinct Caralynne possessed screamed

against the idea of summoning her daughter to join this chase, but it was her duty. She'd have to learn fast.

"She's in St. John's for dinner with Stephanie and Strong... at the Ivory Wharf," Caralynne answered stiffly. "Have someone call her... she can guard the warehouse."

Jimmy had no problem detecting his friend's anxiety, and he considered what she was suggesting. Of course it made sense to have a Champion guarding vital areas on the base... but Alex was in just her second day, and this was an unprecedented danger. So, no.

"Not this time," the Viscount said firmly, and at first Caralynne didn't seem to understand. He thus clarified: "I'll have her warned, but she can stay in St. John's... secure downtown."

The chances of Emily going somewhere so public seemed remote... which, Caralynne rapidly realized, was the point. Alex got to stay out of harm's way one last time.

"Thank you," she said to her friend, and Devlin nodded, then waved with his Thompson towards the ground below.

"Go on, time's wasting."

"Tell Smith," she added quickly, and then she leapt over the rail.

Jimmy watched her disappear in a blur, then took a deep breath and turned back to his office.

Emily was loose in Newfoundland...

CHAPTER XV

The Ivory Wharf was without peer in St. John's. Hugely popular with social notables, the place claimed the best cuisine on the island of Newfoundland, and entertained enough egos on a regular basis for some people to actually believe that boast was true.

Most sensible people understood that the cooking at a place like the Caribou Hut was, in fact, much better — largely because Newfoundland cooks usually believed that a plate needed to be full in order for something to be called a meal. At the Ivory Wharf, the chef seemed to want to show off the whiteness of the fine china more than his own talents, so he often confined his French-styled dishes to a very small and unsatisfying portion of the plate.

This tendency was the reason Alex never liked the Wharf — she was a young Champion with a big appetite, and she expected a good feed whenever she sat down at a table. Still, it was both polite and expected for a new Lady and her lance to visit the Wharf for a meal soon after joining the regiment — sort of a sociable coming-out, though some made far more of a fuss over it than others.

Alex just wanted to get this pilgrimage out of the way,

and because Stephanie had no more enthusiasm for the Wharf than her friend, she was equally inclined to get in and out fast... then go and find a second supper elsewhere on Water Street.

Both girls' intentions were, unfortunately, at odds with the appetites of their Sergeant. Mike Strong was enjoying the sophisticated atmosphere far too much: "I've always dreamed of getting thrown out of a place like this!"

They were waiting on their food — not only were the portions small, but they took a very long time to be delivered — so Stephanie was sipping a glass of water when the Colour made his declaration. Lowering her glass, she shrugged at him, "Don't know if you're good enough for that. They might ask you to throw yourself out."

"Ah yes. You can tell the place is fancy when they ask you instead of telling you," Strong countered, and Stephanie smiled.

After a long day of rover-driving, all three of the new team were running low on fuel; the food, what little of it was to be served, would be most welcome. Until it arrived, Alex didn't expect she'd have enough mental stamina for witty jabs, so instead she stared out the restaurant's large windows. Water Street was lighting up now that the sun had set; electric lights were glowing all around, casting the rover parked just beyond the restaurant with a yellow hue. Across the way, the Bowring Brothers store shone as well, all its fine wares on display in its big window displays.

In one of those displays was a white coat... too long for the young Champion, but it did make her think: should she buy a second one for training abuse, and work in the field, so she didn't have to be so careful? She contemplated the idea, wondering whether the coat she now wore would take any offense, and as her silence endured the eager Sergeant sitting opposite her moved on to other amusements.

"So we have 'what would Mike Strong do?' and 'the legend of whitecoat'. What novelty should we set aside for our fine Lieutenant Shylock?" he asked, and though Alex was largely tuned out, Stephanie shook her head.

"I think I can do without the epithet, Colour. Truly."

"Come on now, it's a bonding experience. We all prove our humor is bad, and that we don't care that it's bad. That makes this lance a safe place for all of us, and it gives us bad jokes to fall back on in times of stress," the Sergeant explained, but his young Lieutenant just frowned.

"Bad jokes help in times of stress? I suppose I can sort of see that..."

Strong nodded, "Oh they do. You call back a joke from months before, and then you... um."

The Sergeant's words trailed off abruptly, and for a moment Stephanie wondered if she was missing a punch line. But as Strong's expression slowly tightened, and his eyes started looking faraway, her frown deepened, "Colour?"

"Old or round, George...?" he barely breathed the question, then sat back in his chair. His gaze remained distant, until he closed his eyes.

By now Alex had noticed the change in Strong's mood, and turning away from the window she frowned, "You okay, Colour?"

He didn't seem to hear the question — his eyes screwed tightly shut, and he clenched his jaw. This clearly was no act — no joke in the making — so Alex and Stephanie shared a concerned glance.

"Colour, do you need help..." Stephanie leaned forward, wondering if her Sergeant had begun to feel unwell. He still didn't answer, which was even more concerning.

And then he opened his eyes. He didn't look right at either Alex or Stephanie, but they could both see his gaze was glassy, and his eyes bore a great sadness. For another dozen seconds he remained silent, then he swallowed and shook his head.

"You just call back the joke. It... um..." he was no more capable of finishing that thought — of remembering James Devlin's last words to the dying Major George Tucker — than he had been the first time, so he forced himself to stop trying.

Again a memory had snuck up on him, taken him right back to the day his regiment had been nearly annihilated. It was embarrassing, but he couldn't afford to dwell on that — he had to get himself out of this conversation. The mood would pass... it always did... but he could give it a nudge along. The waiter had already brought wine, so while he was accustomed to stronger fare, the Colour decided to empty his glass of the overly-sweet red stuff.

It was a telling sign for both his watchers, and with her frown deepening, Alex assumed a tone that was surprisingly maternal, "Alright, Colour?"

"Just... gas..." he lied. "I'll be all set soon."

It sounded as though he was trying to convince himself more than his audience, but sharing another glance, neither Stephanie nor Alex knew whether they should press the question further.

There was plenty about the Colour that was different than his reputation would have suggested, but in itself, that divergence wasn't terribly interesting. People were often different than they were made out to be.

The more worthy question in Strong's case was *who* had built his reputation... and for what purpose. Did Mike Strong need people to believe he was something he didn't think he was?

That wasn't a question to which either Stephanie or Alex expected an immediate answer — there'd be plenty of time in the field when they could seek insight into their trusty Sergeant. For now it seemed he needed to get away from his own thoughts, and Alex decided to make a suggestion on that front.

"Why don't you go out for a little air, Colour?" she asked softly. Then, to make sure it didn't sound too serious, she added: "I promise I won't eat all your food if it comes before you get back."

Stephanie caught on immediately to her friend's intent, and added levity of her own, "Notice her wording: she plans to eat *some* of your food. But still, go get some air."

Strong didn't manage to look at either girl — his eyes were pointed safely away, where the horrors that filled them could harm neither youngster. Mike had hardly been their age when he'd made the charge with Waller...

He shut his lids again. Air was a very good idea, and before he got lost in another cycle of memory, the Sergeant nodded, "Just leave me some potatoes."

With that he left the table, and both Stephanie and Alex watched him go. After he stepped out the door, the Champion looked to her Lieutenant, and their frowns were nearly identical. There was plenty left to learn about Mike Strong.

When Caralynne burst out of the trees at the Torbay Airport, she found the entire massive field was flooded with light. The Royal Newfoundland Regiment had turned out in force, and though the b'ys who filled the ranks of the rock's famed national formation weren't quite so handpicked as the men of the Special Service Regiment, they were damned good soldiers.

As soon as Caralynne appeared out of the woods, she heard the call: "Who goes there?"

Knowing that Emily was the threat, the b'ys watching

the perimeter from their machine gun posts were keyed up to receive someone of Caralynne's build, so she held up both hands and replied, "Lady Caralynne, here to reinforce you."

"Sounds like you, M'Lady, but walk up here slowly so we can see it's you!" came the call back — it sounded like Captain Bragg, one of the RNR's Company commanders.

Without too much haste, or too little speed, Caralynne crossed the clear grassy field from the treeline towards the skycruiser hangers, and the nearer she got, the more b'ys she saw. The Regiment was fully deployed — Colonel Gallway, another veteran of the new world (though he'd been in a Canadian regiment at the time) knew how important it was to be ready when someone like Emily was the threat.

Now Caralynne spotted the Colonel advancing from the aircruiser hangers, and he reached Captain Bragg's rover just before she arrived there.

"It's truly Emily?" Gallway's question was severe, and she nodded.

"Nearly shot Jimmy, killed at least one man in her escape. We figure she's looking for Saa machinery, and needs to get off the island, so she may be coming this way next."

Pulling off his beret, Gallway shook his head, "Well I'm sorry to hear that. Must be rough on you, seeing her so out of sorts."

It wasn't easy, but Caralynne didn't want to get into a conversation about her feelings at just this moment. Instead she nodded to the hangers, "The cruisers are secure?"

Gallway nodded, "All doors are bolted save the one in and out of the side office, and that's covered by three Bren guns... and then the office door's covered by three more. She'll have a hell of a time if she tries to come through."

That was good — there was no question that Emily was a match for any dozen men from the RNR, but she couldn't walk through walls... at least not without enough of a racket to give the b'ys a chance to deploy to stop her. With only one way in, and low ceilings in the office so she couldn't jump, it was safe to say the hangers were secure.

"Thing is," Gallway continued while Caralynne mused on the arrangements, "I wouldn't expect her to come this way. Unless she's learned to fly skycruisers, or even just planes, we don't have a good way off the island. She could capture a pilot, I suppose... but she'd have to know we'd button the place right up tight. Why not just go steal a boat somewhere?"

Caralynne had begun to scan the open airfield... it really was bathed in floodlights, impossible to cross without at least being seen. The skycruisers were certainly the most valuable machines in Newfoundland, and for that reason they were quite well-protected... so if Emily had planned to escape after robbing Jimmy of whatever printouts he could provide, a boat would be very sensible — perhaps just a small craft that would take her out to sea for a rendezvous with a Mothership.

Very sensible, and Caralynne allowed herself some self-scolding for not already thinking of it. She'd been too distracted fearing for her daughter — not that she should be ashamed of such worries.

So if Emily was going for a boat, where would she try? On an island like Newfoundland, there seemed far too many possibilities… she could go to any cabin with a dory tied up off shore, any outport…

Or she could go to the biggest collection of boats in Newfoundland. The harbor in St. John's had plenty to choose from, though it was also very public, and there was a Royal Navy destroyer in port. Chances seemed slim that the rogue Lady would take such risks… but then, she'd hardly been discrete in New York.

Something else Caralynne realized she should have thought of sooner. She and Jimmy had expected Alex to be safer in St. John's, but…

Caralynne needed to find her daughter. If Emily got away through some secluded cove, that would be a shame. But Alex was more important.

"Telephone Headquarters and tell Jimmy I'm going to check the harbor… make sure everything is okay there."

"Will do," Gallway nodded, and with that Caralynne disappeared back into the trees.

Mike Strong was taking deep breaths as he leaned against his trusty rover. With his arms folded and a focus on getting cool night air into his lungs, he began to feel some of his dark mood uncoil. Watching his two girls helped. They were inside the Ivory Wharf, looking quite serious, and he figured they might be able to see him staring. But they were pretending not to notice.

It was important for him to look, though. Now, more than ever before, he had a good reason to keep his head clear. He'd always focused on being a good soldier, and looking out for his men. He'd caused himself grief at times, and had done his share of bad behavior, but mostly he'd been trying to live right because there'd been too many b'ys who'd surrendered that chance.

He was lucky to be alive, and he wanted to make sure he acted like it.

Now, though, he was responsible for two people, and they were responsible for him. It was important that he didn't let them down on either front, and that meant he needed to keep his moods under control. Silly memories couldn't get in the way of him doing what was best, or listening when he was told to act.

Alex and Stephanie were going to be depending on him, and that mattered. Watching both those youngsters, Strong focused his mind, and continued shaking the grim thoughts that had crept up on him.

Then he got unwanted help.

"Pretty lassies. I suppose this warrants the question: *which one* would Mike Strong do? I'll have the other, unless you want both at once."

Bosun McKenna, from the destroyer *Inglefield*, strode up beside the Sergeant with a big grin. Behind him, seven of his lads were coming along, all clearly bound for a pub where they could get a good start to the night.

Strong couldn't tell if that introduction was meant to be friendly or to restart the brawl from two days earlier. Nor did he much care, because the Irishman was speaking of Alex and Stephanie in a way that was not right.

"I swear I heard you say something, McKenna," Strong didn't look in the Irish sailor's direction as he spoke, and the bosun laughed a bit more harshly.

"If your hearing's going, how'll you know whether the girls like it?"

Some would say it was just sailor's talk. In a different place and a different time it might have been harmless. At this particular moment, however, Mike Strong asked himself his question.

There would be a fight.

CHAPTER XVI

"Oh... Oh!" Stephanie had been pretending not to notice Colour Strong's intense stare, but when the sailors showed up her observation of the Sergeant had become less subtle. "Fight!"

Alex looked up at the warning, just in time to see Strong grab a big-looking sailor by his collar and wind up for a swing. It was impossible to say precisely why he was getting ready to take on eight of the Royal Navy's finest single-handedly — there was too much ambient noise in the restaurant for her to hear outside — but it didn't matter.

Their food hadn't even arrived yet, but they were going to back up Mike Strong... hungry or not, he was their responsibility.

Pushing herself to her feet, Alex vaguely noticed that the restaurant telephone had begun to ring, but ignored it. Before Stephanie could even get clear of the table, Lady Smith was outside.

Mike Strong tried to punch the bosun in the middle of his face, but just as he was about to launch his fist, he discovered it was stuck in cement. Or, at least, that's how it felt — and then he realized he could feel fingers closed around his wrist.

"What's all this, Colour?" Alex had a stern frown on her face, but Strong wasn't quite ready to answer a sensible question.

The bosun started to grin — started to puff up with a comment about how the Newfoundlander always seemed to have women come along to save him from beatings — but then he realized the significance of the serious-looking girl who'd arrived.

McKenna had never seen a Champion wearing white, but this young girl certainly did appear to be a Lady, and that made things seem a lot worse to the sailor.

Stephanie wasn't far behind, and as a girl in battle dress with Lieutenant's pips on her shoulders stepped out into the electrically-lit night, the bosun and his fellow *Inglefields* seemed to blanch. Not a whole lot about St. John's was making sense to them.

"Now Strong, you know it was just in fun," McKenna turned his eyes back to his fisticuffs opponent, but the Sergeant gave no indication, verbal or otherwise, that he believed that.

"Colour, let him go for now. We can beat him if he deserves it but my hand is getting tired," Alex interrupted, doing her best to match the authority she'd heard in her mother's voice when circumstances warranted. She did a pretty fair job of that, and the words succeeded in piercing the Sergeant's personal fog.

Feeling the force behind the intended punch waning, Alex gently loosened her grip on the Colour's arm, then took a step back. Gradually, the Sergeant did the same.

As he disengaged, the bosun eased back towards his lads, then waved to them to start their departure — better they be gone in case Strong spilled some of their talk to the whitecoat and her officer.

Unfortunately, the girl Lieutenant was very sharp: "You men stop there. I want to know what's going on."

Stephanie was projecting artificial authority, just as Alex was. Of course both young ladies knew how to speak their minds, and command their own actions, but there was a certain dry timber... an almost aristocratic disdain... that they mimicked to give their words power over others. Now the bosun winced at the order to stay, but decided it was best to try to talk his way out of the mess. Running away would just get him caught, because Strong would give up his name.

"Ma'am," the Irishman said, turning towards the very pretty Lieutenant who had the American accent. "It was just a misunderstanding... we had a go, Strong and me, a couple of days ago over a young lady."

Alex took a step in front of Strong as he bristled at McKenna's words, then pointed her question at the bosun, "You were accosting that young lady, sailor?"

The Irishman's eyes widened, and he looked properly

incredulous, "Of course not. I mean, may have had a bit too much of a pat of her leg, but that was just innocent fun. Never would put myself upon a lady."

Stephanie approached the bosun as he spoke, "So the Colour took you out to the woodshed for some poor conduct. And you wanted revenge?"

"I just made a joke to him, is all," the Irishman shook his head, getting a bit flustered.

"About the same girl?" Alex advanced another step, and suddenly McKenna found himself being assaulted on two sides by girls young enough to be his daughter, about whom he'd thoughtlessly made a bad joke in order to needle a soldier he had half a mind to beat. There was obviously a lesson to be learned from this, and the bosun could only hope he survived to forget it.

Fortunately for the *Inglefield*, help was at hand: "What the devil is all this?"

Alex and Stephanie paused simultaneously, then both looked back to see none other than Captain Todd emerging from the Ivory Wharf, wearing his dress blues and looking rather displeased that his supper had been disrupted.

"You were in the restaurant?" Alex asked abruptly, her frown deep.

Todd stopped in surprise, "Yes, obviously…"

"Why didn't I notice you?"

"That… hardly seems material. What's this, another fight with your man Strong?"

Alex had no idea of the context of that comment, and neither did Stephanie. But they both knew they didn't like the Royal Navy Captain who doubted Stephanie's right to her uniform.

"Seems that your man was trying to cause trouble with our Sergeant," Stephanie turned fully back towards Todd, just in time to see a nervous-looking waiter emerge from the Ivory Wharf behind the Captain.

"We'll see about that," the Briton became instantly defensive, and that clouded Stephanie's expression further.

Alex turned after her friend, "Captain, I don't know what you consider appropriate conduct, but this hardly creates a good impression. I would have expected more from the senior service than harassing a veteran of the Hubrin War."

"Now see here," Todd strode forward again, his eyes fixed on Lady Alex, his natural authority beginning to assert itself. It would be quite a challenge to—

"I overheard the entire thing. Allow me to resolve this fairly."

From nowhere the voice cut into the night, and even though the woman who spoke was just feet from McKenna, the bosun hadn't seen her arrive. He also didn't quite see as she drew a Colt 1911 from beneath her cloak, pointed it at the center of his forehead, and squeezed the trigger.

The Irishman fell dead against the side of the rover before Stephanie or even Alex was able to turn. Todd's mouth fell open and his eyes widened, "Who the hell are—"

Alex managed to dive into him before the bullet would have cracked his chest open, and as the sailors who'd been with McKenna scattered in panic, the woman turned and began to summarily execute them — six fell before her magazine ran dry, suggesting she'd had one round in the chamber before she'd begun shooting.

Reloading after that, Emily began to pivot back towards Todd.

"You know who I am," she said, completing her turn.

And then she found herself looking down the barrels of two Browning Hi-Powers, and a Thompson submachine gun that Strong had somehow retrieved from the arms box in the rover.

"Emily," the Sergeant greeted her sharply.

Caralynne hurdled through the dark Newfoundland woods with all the speed and sure-footedness she could manage. She needed to get downtown, just in case Emily was there — just in case the woman who'd once been her sister now tried to kill her daughter.

But in the low light, even Caralynne's Champion eyes were having trouble with the underbrush. She was only a few miles away — a distance that, on the grasslands of the new world, would have been covered in no time at all... but she was being slowed down by the dense forest of the island.

She prayed that she would arrive and find nothing

amiss… just her daughter dining at a pretentious restaurant.

It was as she held onto that hope that Caralynne ran straight into a bull moose, bowling the poor fellow over, and knocking herself onto the ground in a stunned state.

"Is no one going to shoot me on sight?" Emily's question was almost coy, and she smiled as three guns all bore down on her.

It was possible that three shooters would be too many for her — that even if she got one or two of them, the third might manage to make a bullet touch her, even if just to slow her down. But no one was shooting.

Alex knew who she was pointing her Browning at. It didn't make any sense — the waiter carrying the telephone warning from Fort Waller had gone back inside to hide — but this was certainly Lady Emily. She vaguely remembered the woman from her childhood, and of course she'd seen photos since.

Stephanie's recognition was also driven by pictures; where Emily had been part of Alex's very young life, the American girl had grown up on the frontier, and had heard only stories of the first Champion and her wild ways.

Strong recognized the rogue Lady best of all, because he'd been there on the new world — had marched with her and fought savages alongside her.

All three of them had their guns pointed squarely at Emily's chest, and the woman's own Colt was down at her side. Theoretically, it could all be ended in this instant…

"Someone *shoot* her," Todd was scrambling back to his feet with that order, and his perspective on this was entirely clear: at least seven of his men had been shot, one certainly to his death.

"Shut up, Captain," Alex barked back immediately, surprised by the coarseness in her tone.

Only slowly was the young Lady's mind catching up to everything her body was doing: she had drawn her pistol and thumbed off its safety… then pointed it and lowered herself into a proper shooting crouch… then positioned herself to be equidistant between Strong on her left and Stephanie on her right…

Everything she was supposed to do, she'd done in a blink. And now she was beginning to process that Emily, who undoubtedly had attacked the train in New York, was here in St. John's, standing beside the rover, on the sidewalk, having shot people.

"You're too wise to shoot one of your own kind, Alexandra," Emily's smile was sinister. "Yes, I remember you from when you were little… though you haven't grown as tall as I would have thought. And you are very skinny."

Alex blinked — those words were clearly meant to get under her skin, but why?

"And Stephanie, I've read of you, of course. Your uncle saved my life, so it would be wrong of me to kill you. But that's the only reason you might survive this encounter we're sharing today."

Stephanie's brow creased deeply at that: an insult of her abilities meant to trigger an irresponsible reaction? The young American redoubled her glare down the sights of her Browning, and made sure she was ready to shoot.

But would they shoot? Emily had given them plenty of reason to, but somehow they couldn't.

It was Emily. She had been a kind of family...

"Mike Strong. I remember you too, of course. You still pretending to be a brave womanizer, when you're just a broken little boy?"

That similarly crude and unkind assault on the Colour netted nothing but a more confident glare from him; his mood had passed — been driven away by the adrenaline in his veins.

"I'm just asking myself a question, Lady Emily..." the Colour cut through the torment with his words, and hearing the steel underlying his tone, both Alex and Stephanie found their minds beginning to settle again. Then he asked, "What would Mike Strong do?"

It was plainly a stupid question, but as a quizzical look formed on Emily's brow, the Colour was able to move forward, leading with his Thompson as he got nearer the rogue Lady. This was not something she would have resisted anyway — letting soldiers close just made it easier for her to snap their necks without shooting — but as she realized the question probably wasn't meant to make sense, the rogue

Champion took note of his approach.

Unsure of his intentions, she then leapt back a dozen paces in a single elegant jump, her Colt still down at her side, "What are you doing?"

"That's what I just asked," Strong answered, crouching at the end of the rover and then putting one knee on the ground. "Looks to me like you're worried."

Emily didn't know what was happening — and that was perhaps because no one else did either. But where she was waiting to respond to some threat, Alex and Stephanie were both looking to their Sergeant, realizing that by his sheer wit he'd managed to push Emily back far enough that her fists were out of instant range.

He'd gained distance for them.

"Shoot her, dammit!" Todd hurried forward to the rover, then reached into the arms box — which Strong had left open when he retrieved his Thompson — and pulled out a Garand.

Alex advanced past Strong in a flash, her Browning still up but her back between Todd and Emily, effectively blocking his shot, "You're here looking for something... same as you were in New York. What are you after? Who are you working with?"

The questions spilled out of the young Champion, again mostly by instinct — she recalled what she and her mother had discussed about Snapdragon, and hoped now it was right to ask about.

Emily considered Alex through narrowed eyes, then noticed Stephanie cast a quick glance at Strong, drawing the Sergeant to his feet. He then darted left, out past the rover and onto Water Street, which was fortunately devoid of traffic. Stephanie moved up the sidewalk to Alex's right — perfect spacing selected instinctively by an American girl who's godfather was a gunfighter.

Seeing all the movement to envelop her, Emily simply smiled, "You three would all be dead if I didn't have reason to keep you alive. Captain Todd will be dead if he doesn't put down his rifle. And Alexandra, I will not speak to you of my position until you open your mind to the prospect I might, in fact, be correct."

That sounded to Stephanie much like the declarations of the racist speaker from the pub, and she said as much: "Awfully sure of yourself."

"Just as you are. The difference being that I'm correct."

"Of course," Alex interjected darkly. "Then you'll drop your pistol and join us in a visit to Fort Waller. Where you will explain yourself, and since you're right, we'll all feel enlightened and join your cause."

Emily's smile broadened, "Don't be so confident you wouldn't, Alexandra. But that's not for today. I have other priorities until…"

Her words trailed off as Todd hurried up behind Alex with his Garand. Seeing the recognition of a target in the rogue Champion's expression, the Lady in white turned quickly enough to catch the Captain raising the rifle, then with a quick lunge she dove back into him, knocking the weapon away.

Before she could turn back, she knew Emily would launch herself into the air, and disappear…

But the Thompson cut out.

Strong's firing was a surprise — he hadn't shot before, why now? But Stephanie, who was parallel to him on the street, suddenly realized what he was doing: his shots were going over Emily's head, preventing the Lady from leaping away to safety.

Wrapping her second hand around the grip of her Browning for added stability, Stephanie then locked Emily's Colt straight in her sights, and squeezed the trigger.

The shot would have done Cameron Kard proud: it clipped the barrel of Emily's 1911, and knocked it from her hand. A very fine feat, even from fifteen yards kneeling.

Staggering back a couple of steps, Emily lowered herself into a more proper fighting crouch, her expression losing all of its previous humor. Strong held his fire — he had established that he'd shoot high if she tried to move, so the rules were clear. She was trapped in a box of fire, and her only way out would be to distract one or both of the guns pointed at her.

That… she could do.

With a powerful swing of her arm, Emily sent her cape flying upward. Seeing only a blur and knowing he couldn't hope to follow the full-speed launch of a veteran Champion, Strong cut loose with his Thompson... but with only fifteen rounds left of the thirty that had been in his magazine, he ran dry fast.

Before he realized he'd been decoyed.

Riddled with holes, the cape started to fall to the street... but not before Emily was upon the Sergeant. He knew she was coming for a whole second before she arrived, and he swung his hot Thompson in what he figured was the direction she'd come from, using the heavy gun as a club since he hadn't grabbed anything else from the arms box.

Emily's boot drove into his stomach, then her fist crossed his jaw. Never in his life had Mike Strong been struck harder, and the blows tossed him through the front window of the Bowring Brothers store. Fortunately the display behind him was of clothing and not knives; he dropped inside the display case with a wheeze, trying to remember what his name was.

As soon as the move happened, Stephanie Shylock knew she had to displace. Alex was just getting back to her feet after tackling the Captain, so someone had to keep Emily occupied until she could rejoin the fight.

Shooting on the run, one-handed and with a mind towards not squeezing the trigger unless she was certain there were no bystanders behind her target who could be harmed by her fire, the young Lieutenant hurried out into the street.

Emily was very, very fast though — and charging closer to Stephanie with every incredible leap.

Stephanie emptied her magazine just as fast as the rogue Lady was able to move, but there was no way to hit anything — no way to provide more than a distraction.

"Alex!" Stephanie called as soon as her Browning's slide locked back, and the young Champion regained her feet just in time to watch Stephanie be catapulted up high into the air — to an altitude from which she surely couldn't fall without being harmed.

No choice: Alex leapt into the night right behind her friend, wrapped her arms around her, and together they came down in as orderly a fashion as was possible. The two girls' boots hit the ground first, but without the ability to distribute both their weights by herself, Alex couldn't keep them upright. She ended up falling on Stephanie... which was probably best, as she was the lighter of the pair.

But Emily's blows had knocked the wind right out of the Lieutenant, so as she struggled to make her lungs function, Alex leapt to her feet and leveled her Browning again... only to discover that Emily was nowhere to be seen.

Quickly she turned, looked back behind the rover, then down the street again, then up... no sign.

So she listened carefully... listened for any sound of movement...

Boots were clapping along, but from above. She was crossing the roofs of the downtown buildings, heading north.

Looking down at Stephanie, who was trying to force her lungs to work, and then across at Strong, who was sitting up inside the clothing display, Lady Alex Smith made a quick decision: "I'm going after her... northward. Follow when you can!"

She leapt into the sky, and left her ordinary guardians behind.

CHAPTER XVII

Stephanie could hardly breathe when she managed to get to her feet. Alex's message rang in her ears — *north* and *follow* — but she didn't have a sense of how long it had been since her friend had given chase. She tried to grasp the answer to that question as she staggered across the road, heaving as best she could to get air into her lungs, and found her Browning which had been lying on the tarmac.

As she bent down to get her fingers around the pistol, she started to feel as though some oxygen was flowing back into her brain. She straightened a bit more steadily, looked across the street to see Colour Strong forcing himself out of the display in the Bowring Brothers' window, and figured that meant he was alive.

Emily hadn't killed either of them. She hadn't had her pistol — Stephanie vaguely recalled taking care of that — but still, there was no question the savage-born woman... perhaps just a 'savage' now... was fully capable of tearing them apart. Either she really wouldn't kill Stephanie because of Uncle Bo's rescue twenty years prior, or Alex had chased her off.

Closing her eyes as her head started hurting, Stephanie

tried to think. North immediately... they had to get after Alex...

"Lieutenant, you can most certainly expect that I will report this mess to your commanding officer. You *let her escape*," Captain Todd sounded agitated, and his outburst cut through the fog in Stephanie's mind.

Her answer was reflective of her dislike for the man, "Excuse me?"

Opening her eyes, she expected the dandy of a British Captain to be prancing around and lecturing her as though somehow he knew what he was talking about. Instead she turned and found him trying to stop the bleeding from the wound suffered by one of his men... the only one of his men who Emily had shot but not killed.

In his dress blues, kneeling on the road and using his handkerchief to try to keep an ordinary seaman from dying, he was hardly a picture of aristocratic ignorance. But that didn't make him right.

"Dammit all," he spat the words as he checked his man for a pulse, but found nothing. With a shake of his head, he closed the fallen man's eyes with his fingers, then stood slowly and turned to Stephanie.

"That woman killed *my crew*, dammit. You had your chance and you shot the pistol from her hands? What bloody piece of theater do you think this is, Lieutenant? I knew it when I saw you in the Fort, and I know it now: you are in no way fit to be an officer. By God, *shot the pistol*? You could have brought her down, but you let her escape? This is no game…"

He was clearly beyond angry and his control over his sentiments was virtually non-existent. Whether he had a point… Stephanie didn't care.

"Do you even realize who that was?" she found her voice all of a sudden. "Emily — *Lady* Emily. Do you think your men here are the extent of the harm she's done? She killed a Champion in New York, and policemen with him. She was after the plans for Snapdragon, and if she's here, that means she's up to something that might well endanger all of us. And you wanted me to shoot her down because she killed some of *your* men? Without the chance for us to interrogate her?"

There was reason to her argument as well, but Todd wasn't hearing it — he was a Captain possessed in the moment by the loss his crew had just suffered, "Because she is a Champion, she is treated differently?"

"You'd have me shoot her on the spot because she's a Champion, wouldn't you? Otherwise you'd have ordered me to take her into custody!"

Both of them were past reason, and Todd took two steps toward Stephanie, his fists clenched. It was two steps too many: Stephanie's sights were lined up on his forehead almost immediately.

"Damn you," he breathed. "Threatening a superior officer? Are you remotely aware of how foolish you are?"

Stephanie's eyes hardened, and she moved her thumb to cock the hammer, only to realize that the Browning's slide was locked back — she hadn't yet reloaded. With a frustrated shake of the head, she reached into her pocket for a fresh magazine, and Todd took another step forward.

Fortunately, a hand landed on his chest, and another pushed down Stephanie's gun, "Where's Alex?"

There was a grim clarity — and a note of physical pain — in Strong's tone, and Stephanie blinked before managing to answer, "North... we need to go north..."

Suddenly her mind started working. Dear God, how long had it been now? And how far had they gone?

"We need to go *north*," urgency suddenly flooded her voice, and as she quickly swapped magazines, her eyes turned in that direction. It was fully dark now, and there was no way to know how much of a head start the two Ladies had. There was also no reason they'd have followed a road...

How could they find Alex? Stephanie's anger transformed into panic, and this was reflected in her face as she realized she'd let her friend get away... what the hell was Alex thinking? And why had she gotten so distracted, and why...?

Strong filled Stephanie's field of vision all of a sudden, crouching slightly so he could meet her gaze as he put his hands on her shoulders: "This is what it's like. This is what happens when you start getting to war. Things don't make sense in your head, and only some people know how to deal with that. You are one of those kind. You're smarter than me. Don't doubt it, just trust that I'm right. Now tell me where we have to go."

That was all a good Sergeant needed to know: officers were supposed to decide where to be, and NCOs were the ones who figured out how to get them there. There were many different shades to that relationship, but those were its fundamental principles.

"North," Stephanie whispered to Strong, struggling with his question, then asked one of her own. "What would you do... if you were Emily, what would you be doing coming to St. John's?"

Mike Strong blinked, then looked eastward. He couldn't see the waterfront, but it was not so far away... and it was the only reason he could imagine showing up in this city if he were the most wanted criminal in the British Empire.

"A ship," he said, and Stephanie's mind accepted the word.

"She didn't expect us to be here... she's come to meet a ship. We go north... maybe the lower battery. She might intend on stealing a dory and getting out through the narrows..." as her mind slipped into gear, Stephanie turned away from Strong and stabbed her finger at Todd. "She might be trying to get out through the harbor. We need light... searchlights, star shells... help us find them!"

Todd looked from Stephanie to Strong, then back with

a shake of his head, "Damn you both..."

Then he left. Neither knew where precisely he was headed, or for what purpose, but they didn't have time to pursue. He'd either help or he wouldn't — right now they had to get after Alex and Emily.

Who knew how far they'd gone...

Caralynne lay back for a moment, realizing there was pain radiating from her shoulder, but unsure what it meant. It was a secondary concern: with speed that she should have been able to replicate but for some reason couldn't, the moose had gotten back on his feet. As the dark shape loomed over her, Caralynne realized the danger he presented — he couldn't be pleased, and he was libel to trample her, a threat even a Champion had to respect.

She began to roll away, but that act was made difficult by her left arm not properly responding to commands. Her shoulder had to be dislocated... that was not going to be any help at all...

Approaching her gravely, the moose lowered its antlers as if to ram her, and with a hiss of discomfort Caralynne pushed herself back. A log dug into her, but she had to retreat. The moose stayed still, then looked up slightly and saw that she'd backed off. He took a step forward, and then another, putting his antlers right over Caralynne's chest... then he jerked his head up slightly, and snorted.

Which made no sense. Caralynne was no naturalist, but

she hardly would have expected a bull moose to be under-standing, let alone helpful, when he got bowled over in the middle of the night by a racing Champion.

But there was a saying about gift horses... perhaps it extended to gift moose?

Raising her working arm, Caralynne grasped the moose's antler with her hand, and suddenly he raised his head high. Up she went, onto her feet.

It was terribly good of the big fellow, and Caralynne had no idea why he was being so accommodating... but she nodded to the powerful animal, and he snorted before wandering off.

If she'd had the chance to wonder, she might have really questioned that moose intervention... but there was no time. Alex might be facing Emily, and so her mother raced through the dark woods toward St. John's, hoping she'd arrive in time.

There was no question that Emily was fast. Alex was just managing to keep the elder Lady in sight as they sprinted over downtown St. John's, leaping from rooftop to rooftop illuminated barely by the moon and backlit by the electric lights from the town and the ships in harbor. Still heading north, towards the lower battery and its many small fisherman's homes, she could only assume that the savage woman intended to seize a boat, and make her way out through the Narrows.

Hopefully Stephanie and Strong would be along soon to help prevent that... for now Alex kept up the chase.

From above, the well-protected harbor at St. John's might have been compared to a diagram of a human lung — both shared an oblong shape with a very slender conduit leading out. In the harbor's case, that conduit was known simply as the Narrows, and along what would be the 'top' of the lung sat the lower battery, a collection of houses built onto the precarious lower slopes of Signal Hill, the 500-foot high headland that dominated the northern side of the harbor.

There would be plenty of dories tied up amongst those houses — small boats that Emily could steal quite easily, and paddle out to the safety of a waiting vessel. Of course, the Lady could have simply dived into the harbor and swum out, but Alex had never dared to go for a dip in St. John's waters — the whole town, and all the ships at anchor, dumped their sewage there. Swimming in it was decidedly inadvisable.

So a dory — a small, innocuous fishing boat like the one Alex had rescued beneath the cliff days prior — had to be Emily's plan now. But she wasn't going to get away.

What Alex was going to do when she caught the rogue Lady, she wasn't quite certain... but she'd find a way to deal with the situation. Perhaps she'd even have help.

Leaping down to the road as she reached the end of downtown's last roof, Alex kept her eyes on the blurring shape ahead. No question that Emily was making for Lower Battery Road, but as she moved away from the electric lights of downtown, it became more difficult to see exactly which way she was headed. Were she to stop in ambush while covered by the shadows of night, on a narrow road running alongside the northern section of the harbor…

Dangerous, but Alex wasn't about to stop. She'd pocketed her Browning for her rooftop chase, in case she had a bad landing, but now that solid ground was underfoot she drew it again, thumbed back the hammer and held it out to the side as she ran. Of course her finger did not rest on the trigger — her father had taught her well — but she was ready to shoot if the need arose.

Into the darkness she sprinted, her eyes narrowing as she tried to focus on every shadow and every glimmer. Her ears were sharply listening too — she could hear her own steps of course, and some sounds of the harbor at night… and far ahead, just a hint of the sound of Emily running.

Alex couldn't afford to slow down, but she was careful to listen — not to keep going too blindly if the sounds of Emily's movement disappeared.

Quickly the distance to the lower battery and its precarious homes was covered. Alex had never actually visited these places, but she knew that the houses clung like mountain goats to a shelf of rock that was, in places, almost as steep as the slopes of the assault courses.

From these homes, a cluster of fishermen made their

living, going out in their boats every day, bringing back their catch and drying it on the wooden racks built out over the waters of the harbor.

A few lights — all looking like oil lamps — were lit amongst those structures as they came into view in the distance, and soon Alex heard the telltale sign of boots on wood. Emily was there... hurrying along a wooden dock... soon to find her escape?

Alex redoubled her speed, though as she followed the narrow road — path really — around another cleft in the rock, and neared the first house of the cluster, she realized how difficult it would be to see her foe. She could hear Emily running, and others probably could too. If someone startled her, made some sort of telling noise, that would help — and since Emily was unarmed, that person might even survive the experience.

But light would be most useful — Alex needed to see, and as she hurried around the first house of the lower battery, she said a silent prayer.

Then the heavens thundered, and night turned to day.

"Jesus, that's Todd," Strong looked up only briefly as he drove the rover fast through the downtown streets.

Inglefield was at anchor in the harbor, and now one of her 4.7-inch guns cut open the night sky, lobbing a star shell high into the air. As the ordnance burst, its bright flare turned night into day over St. John's — at least for as long as its parachute survived and let it burn like a little sun.

Hopefully the light would do Alex some good, but until the rover cleared the buildings of downtown, neither Stephanie nor Strong would be able to see where the young Champion was.

"Fast as we can go?" Stephanie asked softly, but firmly, and Strong nodded.

"Absolutely," he said.

They were going hell-for-leather to find their Lady.

As the star shell hung up over the harbor, Alex refocused her hearing towards the ships. Knowing that illumination must have come from *Inglefield*, she expected to hear sounds of hands on deck, commotion, perhaps boats launching.

She heard all of that — sound carried over water quite well — and she also heard a specific cry: "Look there, on the wharf!"

Alex wasn't on a wharf yet — she was still moving along the rapidly-narrowing path between houses, her Browning leading the way. If someone on the destroyer's quarterdeck had seen movement, it was likely Emily, or an unlucky fisherman looking for the intruder.

Either way, Alex adjusted her attention towards the water and found a place between houses to cut through. She came to a stop behind the corner of a house, then leaned around very carefully to see what she could see.

But the star shell was expended; night returned. She

hoped the destroyer would fire another...

And then suddenly, night turned right into noon. Alex had to raise her free hand to shade her eyes as two of *Inglefield's* powerful search lamps pounded the lower battery with daylight. Then the ship fired again, and a star shell added to the brightness.

Waiting just a second for her eyes to adjust, Alex swung around the corner of the house, raising her Browning as she moved. Sure enough, Emily was ninety yards away, kneeling down on a rickety wooden wharf as she tried to untie a dory.

And she was looking up — first at *Inglefield*, then back at Alex.

"You best stop now!" the young Lady called to her elder. "The whole harbor will be here looking for you. They'll sink you if you take that boat!"

Looking back to the destroyer that was clearly ready for her, Emily nodded, "Perhaps you're right, Alexandra."

Then she leapt from view. Even Alex couldn't quite follow the move — she looked up, hurried out onto a nearer wooden pier and turned back toward the houses, hoping the better angle would reveal some sign of the savage Lady... but she was gone.

Of course she wasn't actually gone, she was just out of sight... and that was worse. Dangerous. Taking a breath, the young Lady recalled her practice — the training her father had impressed upon her since her youngest years. She had to keep her eyes moving... stay calm... look for things that didn't fit...

In this much darkness it wouldn't be easy, but there had to be something — or even a sound...

Alex searched the homes of the lower battery with all her senses, but she was too close to see what she needed to see.

The rover drifted very slightly as Strong hammered its brakes at the end of downtown, but Stephanie still managed to stand up on the passenger side, holding onto the top frame of the windshield as she looked out at the water through narrowed eyes.

Two searchlights from *Inglefield* had converged on the lower battery, and almost as soon as she saw them, they started roving. Perhaps they'd found Emily, but she'd leapt out of sight. Either way, it didn't matter.

"Lower battery!" the Lieutenant called to her Sergeant, and Strong hit the clutch and shifted gears just as one of the lights jumped — went high onto the rock face leading up Signal Hill.

That light beam landed on something, and then the other moved to join it... and then both jumped a bit further up the rock face, as though following a climber moving with incredible speed...

"She's climbing the hill!" Stephanie called down again. "Get us up to Cabot Tower."

The tower was a small stone communication station

built atop Signal Hill — the location from which the first trans-Atlantic wireless signal had been sent, or received (Stephanie could never remember). Now it was home to a very small post run by the Newfoundland military... manned perhaps by one or two men, but in no way prepared for the fight that would come if Emily arrived.

"Get down and hold tight," Strong commanded his officer, and then the rover started running like a Champion up the much more gradual rear approach to the 500-foot summit of the hill.

As the searchlights transitioned to the cliff face, Alex followed with her eyes and did indeed find Emily clinging to the rock. The Lady looked back at her tormentors, then down at her pursuer, and then leapt up higher, escaping from the ring of daylight that had caught her.

But whatever their habits while ashore, the destroyer-men on *Inglefield* were experienced professionals; they judged the range of Emily's leap and had her back in their sights almost immediately.

And then, in the distance, Alex heard the telltale sound of machine guns being primed. Of course Todd would be willing to kill...

Without any time to waste, Alex safetied and pocketed her Browning, then sprinted for the hillside. She was further inland, and some of the slopes before her were marginally more passable than those Emily had forced herself onto...

perhaps she could get to the top first.

Another star shell tore into the air as she went, making it easier for her to find her footing, and then her handholds, as she went up the side of the hill. She moved like a shot, just as smoothly as in all her training, and before she knew it, she was on virtually level ground at an abandoned gun emplacement called the Queen's Battery — a position left over from the nineteenth century.

From there it was a straight run up to the tower, and Alex wasted no time in drawing her Browning again and starting forward at a blurring pace. The spotlights weren't quite all the way up the side of the rock face yet — she would be on level ground to meet Emily when she reached the top...

Or not.

The spotlights were suddenly overlapped on the tower, still a few hundred yards away. Alex didn't slow down, but as she ran she could see two men emerging from the building, one clearly carrying an Enfield. Then she watched as a figure landed on the hilltop ahead of them, then leapt into them.

Both men went down hard, one of them giving up his rifle as he fell. So much for Emily being unarmed.

Alex could only hope that they were still alive, though she had no reason to be optimistic. Emily then came to a stop alongside the tower — now less than 200 yards away — and clearly took a second to look around, before turning with the Enfield and aiming it squarely at the approaching

Champion in the white coat.

All the young Lady had time to do was take to the air; as the first .303 rifle round slashed at her, she leapt through the sky, and prepared for a real fight.

CHAPTER XVIII

Adrenaline was fueling most of Caralynne's steps by the time she staggered into downtown St. John's. The sound of *Inglefield's* guns had been audible for a long way, so she knew something did indeed have to be happening in the town. She could only hope that whatever it was, it somehow didn't include her daughter.

Of course, she knew better than that…

As she staggered onto Water Street, her dislocated arm dragging awkwardly at her side, she could see people coming out of buildings along the road — the light show was obvious to anyone with even a small window, and many were stepping outside to see what it was about.

"Where are they?" Caralynne began to demand that information from anyone she saw, realizing she probably sounded desperate, but not caring.

No one seemed to have that answer, though, until one girl appeared from the Caribou Hut: "The destroyer's lights are all focusing on Signal Hill. Does that mean they're up there?"

Caralynne didn't recognize the girl, but the information certainly seemed sound, so she nodded, "It must."

She didn't pause any longer than was necessary to say that; she needed to get up the hill as quickly as she could. Alex had to be fighting Emily, and that was too dangerous.

The No. 4 Mk. II Enfield was the standard rifle of the Royal Newfoundland Regiment, and though it was cosmetically somewhat different than the Short, Magazine Lee-Enfield the b'ys had carried on the new world in 1919, the weapon was mechanically identical in any way Alex knew to be significant.

That was good news for her as she somersaulted through the air, landed and then launched herself again. The SMLE bolt was the fastest in the world, at least as far as the fighting men of the RNR were concerned, but it was still a bolt — it couldn't fire as fast as a Garand, or obviously a Thompson. That gave Emily little hope of hitting Alex… she couldn't even really get close…

But comforting as that fact might have been to the young Lady in white, she was still realizing that someone skilled was indeed firing live ammunition with the intent of striking her. That was not a feeling she was accustomed to… she had to focus to keep fear from setting in.

The range to Emily was dropping with every leap. The rogue was staying under the electric lights of the Cabot Tower, firing calmly as her pursuer closed the distance, and as a leap took her within fifteen yards, Alex had to wonder why. Escape wasn't easy, but it would have been possible

— why stand pat and fire with the wrong rifle at a target so difficult to hit?

The answer was obvious, but Alex only came to it a few seconds before Emily tackled her in mid-air.

She had been recklessly closing the distance when the savage Lady dropped her rifle and took to the sky, launching herself straight up like a battering ram. With her landing trajectory ruined, Alex dropped at a very bad angle, and there was no worrying now about her coat: she put her arms up to keep her head off the rocks as she went straight in, just managing to hold onto her Browning as the jarring impact rattled her bones.

Emily landed on her feet just a few yards behind, and sensing the danger Alex got one foot under her and pitched herself sideways, partway down a mossy slope. She needed distance, but this time Colour Strong wasn't handy to provide it. The rogue Champion thus leapt after the young one, and realizing escape was no option, Alex raised her Browning and fired half-blind, trying to at least limit her opponent's trajectory.

That worked; Emily dropped to the ground just short of actually landing on her, for fear of being clipped on the way in. Alex adjusted her aim and fired again, but because she could only fire in one direction at a time, aiming low gave Emily room to jump once more. Cursing herself, Alex rolled onto her stomach and used her free hand to push herself up to her feet, then leapt immediately.

She just managed to get past Emily's dropping knee, and as she somersaulted and landed higher up on the hill, she looked back in time to see the elder Lady launch. It was a leapfrog battle, and all Alex could do was stay ahead. She hopped again, this time heading closer to the tower, and Emily bounced and followed... only to land when Alex launched herself away from the structure.

This time, the younger Champion fired off a couple of rounds while in the air, hoping to change Emily's direction once more... but that failed, and worse, it slowed her next leap. As she crouched to jump again, Emily was suddenly in front of her, and her hand found the barrel of the Browning — attempted to wrench the gun from Alex's hand.

Knowing better than to try to pull away, Alex stepped in close to Emily, then struck at the elder woman with her elbow and her knee. One blow landed, the other was blocked, and then a powerful hand snaked down to the inside of Alex's thigh, gripped like a vice, and flipped her upside down.

There was no hope of holding onto the Browning as she was thrown; all Alex managed to do (with an incredible feat of dexterity) was hit the magazine release with her thumb. Because of the violence of the motion, the Hi-Power's magazine slid free and dropped to the ground — something it wouldn't normally do, as Brownings rarely ejected their spent magazines with any force.

But Emily didn't seem to care — she had probably never

fired a Browning, and thus wouldn't know its particular quirks. Even as she twirled violently through the air, Alex hoped that was the truth — it was just about the only advantage she might have when she landed.

The wind was hammered out of young Lady Smith when her ribs slammed into a massive rock. It was a blow that might have shattered the bones of a non-Champion, particularly one as slim as Alex, and even with her strength she found it was like being rammed by a moose.

She wheezed and tried to roll away as Emily advanced on her... but couldn't budge.

"You are spirited, and even skilled, Alexandra. God only knows why you chose white for your coat... foolish child. I'm sure I've ruined it now," she said sharply.

Alex held up a hand, able only to wave and gasp, "Cleaners..."

It was impossibly cavalier, and it made Emily smile, "You have more humor than either of your parents. I think you and I might get along one day, if you don't get yourself killed."

There was still no air inside Alex — or at least not enough for conversation. Emily came to stand over her, Browning hanging down by her side as she shook her head, "One day you'll be embarrassed by all this. One day you'll look back and wonder why you ever resisted me."

Even without wind, that made Alex screw up her face.

"You'll see," the elder Lady assured, shaking her head

and then pausing. There was a vehicle approaching — Alex could hear it from her vantage point on the ground. And it sounded like a rover.

Without another word, Emily crouched down and picked Alex up one-handed. Finding herself vertical with her feet off the ground, the young Lady swiveled her head as best she could... then came face-to-face with the bore of her own Browning.

"Empty," she rasped, and Emily chuckled.

"Nice try."

Of course the magazine had been ejected, but as the savage Lady had demonstrated by firing eight shots from her Colt both in New York and on Water Street, semi-automatic pistols often kept one round in the chamber. Emily had probably confirmed the Browning had one loaded while Alex had been on the ground... so of course the elder Lady was confident that she had a shot to play with.

More than she needed.

Alex didn't resist as Emily pulled her back against her, using her like a human shield as the rover turned up the last steep slope to get onto the flat top of Signal Hill. The vehicle's headlights were shining bright, so by the time it stopped it was impossible for either Champion to see exactly who was inside... until they both hopped out.

Strong had a Thompson at his shoulder; Stephanie had her Browning outstretched, and their determination was obvious as they both advanced.

"Your friends," Emily whispered to Alex. "They might be alright, but don't let them fool you. Most regular humans are not."

It seemed very strange propaganda to Alex — given time, she might be able to piece together the elder Lady's particular agenda, or grudge, but that was hardly her priority now. She let herself hang as limp as possible, even as her lungs filled back up with air and her aching body started to recover some of its strength.

Just had to wait for her moment...

The picture confronting Stephanie and Strong was obviously dangerous: Emily had Alex at her mercy, the Champion's own Browning being the threatening weapon. That immediately struck the American Lieutenant as a problem, and she glanced at Strong and then nodded her head slightly to the left. He took a few steps that way, and she took a few steps to the right, making sure they had sufficient separation between them.

"What are you looking for in this, Lady Emily?" the Sergeant then asked, drawing the rogue woman's gaze.

"I'm leaving here, Mike. If you try to stop me I'll have to shoot young Alexandra."

Stephanie had both hands around the grip of her Browning, ready for the most accurate shot she could manage. But she knew any shot would put Alex at risk, because even if her aim was true, it would be easy for Emily to turn and use her as a shield against the bullet.

Then the Browning in the savage woman's hand caught the light from the rover's headlamps, and revealed it had no magazine. Blinking at the sight, Stephanie shifted her focus to Alex. As soon as their eyes met in silent confirmation, the significance was clear.

"Did Alex tell you what happened today?" Stephanie asked, shifting her gaze back to Emily. "She started her own legend... the legend of whitecoat."

It was obviously an unexpected announcement, and Emily frowned, then immediately looked back to Strong to see if he was attempting some action under the pretense of a flimsy distraction. But the Sergeant hadn't moved — he remained in a crouch, looking at her down the sights of his Thompson.

"Do you know how she did it?" Stephanie persisted, and looking back, Emily pushed her cheek up against the side of Alex's face.

"We didn't have much time to chat."

Stephanie smiled at the reply, then rolled her shoulders very slightly as she prepared to fire. The range was fifteen yards and the target would be big enough... the goddaughter of Cameron Kard was ready to shoot.

As soon as Alex saw that certainty cross her friend's face, she closed her hands around Emily's arm and pulled down with all her strength.

Champion against Champion was like moose against moose, but because Alex was smaller and possessed a slightly lower center of gravity, she was just able to pull her captor off-balance.

It was enough to force Emily to take a step forward, and the savage Lady growled into Alex's ear: "Stupid child!" She then lowered the Browning from Alex's temple and aimed for the girl's thigh, "You'll learn as I did..."

Then she squeezed the trigger.

Alex's heart skipped a beat — she knew, of course, that the reason all the Brownings in Lord Jimmy's Special Service Regiment required tuned triggers was because their factory-installed magazine safeties tended to wreck their trigger pulls. Emily didn't possess the same knowledge — her gun was a Colt, and it had no such mechanism, meaning it would fire a round from the chamber, even if there was no magazine seated.

Not so with the Browning.

No shot cracked out — one round in the chamber, but the magazine safety had done its job.

Now Alex did hers.

Leaning forward, she threw her head back, and in her surprise Emily wasn't ready for the blow. It hit her in the cheek, and she let go of the Browning just as Alex reached for it.

"Quite a lesson for someone..." the young Lady turned fast and drove her boot into her elder's stomach, and as Emily staggered back Mike Strong cut loose with shots over her head.

Then Stephanie Shylock aimed for the Lady's thigh, and fired.

That shot missed — Emily was stunned but not slow. With Strong's bursts of Thompson fire keeping her at ground level, she raced to the left, to the edge of the hill that overlooked the open sea.

Stephanie tried another shot, but this time one-handed as her other hand reached into her pocket and fished out one of her spare magazines. She lobbed that to her friend and Alex caught it in midair, slammed it home, then started shooting too.

Emily dashed left along the rim, then right, and then as Stephanie Shylock came to the last round in her magazine, she gripped her Browning with both hands, lead her target, and squeezed off a perfect shot.

The bullet hadn't been aimed at Emily, but at the point Stephanie figured the woman would move to... and she was right. A 9mm lead ball slammed through the Lady's left calf, and with a yell of dismay she staggered down to one knee.

Firing stopped — Emily was trapped against the rim of the hill, and Alex, Stephanie and Strong all stood off and reloaded as she clutched her wound. None of them wanted to get too close now... whether she was playing possum or was simply wounded, she might be at her most dangerous. Better to be patient and wait until more help was at hand — the whole of St. John's had to know they were up on Signal Hill, so an assault company, or some of *Inglefield's* marines, or Caralynne, would soon turn up.

"You won't kill me," Emily's voice had gone shaky as she slowly and painfully stood, then backed right up to the hill's edge. At once her defiance became clear: the Lady didn't intend to be taken, even if it meant swimming with a gunshot wound.

"Keep her down!" Stephanie called to Strong, and they both raised their weapons expecting a final defiant leap skyward — a launch that would give the savage Lady enough distance to make it safely out over the water.

At the same time, Alex took two steps forward, "Don't be foolish..."

That protest died as soon as her eyes and Emily's met. There was a quiet and yet desperate certainty in the elder woman's gaze, and Alex felt a stab of doubt as she saw it. Something had turned the Lady wrong, but whatever had done it wasn't madness... or not solely madness. There was conviction in her stare, and perhaps even a recognition of the tragedy inherent in her actions.

"Stop me," Emily answered her young counterpart softly, and briefly Alex wondered whether the words were a plea.

But there was no time to ask: instead of leaping, Lady Emily fell straight back off the ledge. With no jump to clear the rocks at the base of the sheer rock face, there was no telling if she could survive the drop, and as Strong and Stephanie lowered their weapons, Alex hurried to the hill's edge to look down for signs of the rogue.

She was greeted by sheer darkness. This side of the hill faced the open sea, not the harbor, so *Inglefield's* lights didn't clarify anything. Waves crashing into rocks below obscured any sounds, so Alex was left with no clues; the woman had simply fallen into darkness.

Clasping Alex's arm as she came up to the ledge for a look of her own, Stephanie shook her head, "That's not something you're going to try, right? Not going to follow her down there?"

Alex blinked a couple of times, then looked at her friend, "I... no. No. Not at all."

"Good," Strong was quickly at her other side, leaning as far forward over the ledge as he dared before taking a step back. "Because a rover can't drive that slope."

Perhaps in other circumstances that would've sounded like an attempt at a joke, but not this time. The Colour was breathing heavily, and as the stress of the fight started to slowly uncoil, he knew his body would soon start to respond. Adrenaline would retreat from his system, pains and aches would start to creep in... he wasn't as young as he'd once been, and he figured he was about to be reminded of that fact.

Turning his back to the sea, he called to his two charges, "Come away from the ledge. The navy can go look for her. You're both about to start feeling very sick, so you better sit down."

Alex turned her eyes back to the darkened ocean one more time, willing herself to see some sign of the savage Lady... then shook herself and turned away, "I think I feel... fine..."

"Me too," Stephanie agreed, but moved back from the ledge with her friend. It was only when she tripped on a weed and nearly fell over that she realized her legs were like rubber.

Fortunately Alex was beside her, and able to keep her on her feet... before the shakes set in.

"Oh my," was all the young Lady could say, before stopping a few yards from the edge of the hill and falling onto her backside. A great sick feeling started to creep up inside her, and knots formed in her stomach.

Dropping onto her knees beside her friend, Stephanie managed to think to empty her pistol before laying it down, then hung her head, "God, I'm glad I didn't get to eat. Otherwise..."

"We'd both be showing gull Casanova how to regurgitate dinner?" Alex asked, her attempt at humor failing to quell the quaking in her own stomach.

Stephanie grimaced, "Is that one of those bad jokes that's supposed to help get us through stressful moments?"

"Told you," Strong confirmed with a sigh. He'd found a large rock to perch on, and after clearing his Thompson he put his hands on his knees and breathed as his body aches came through. Experience in combat had got him past the sort of physical responses the girls were dealing with, but different sorts of pains were causing him discomfort. He'd been thrown through a window, after all.

"Is it always like this after a fight? I couldn't imagine..." Alex breathed shakily as she tried to follow her Sergeant's instructions.

Shaking his head, Strong spoke reassuringly, "Just because you're not used to it. You'll be remembering some of your decisions for a while... second-guessing and realizing how dangerous everything was. That'll take time. For now it's just the adrenaline leaving. And remember, we were all hungry before she showed up, so you're crashing on an empty stomach."

None of that sounded pleasant; both girls just hoped it would pass quickly.

"Well," Stephanie gave up kneeling and flopped onto her side, then decided the ground was soft enough that it might actually be alright to lie down. "I guess... I'm not ready to think about whatever it is we just did."

That sounded fair to Alex, and deciding her friend had the right idea, she fell sideways so they could lie side by side. Together they looked up at the stars, taking deep breaths as the events of the night started to play back before their eyes.

Somewhere in the waters below, Emily swam away.

CHAPTER XIX

Caralynne was two thirds of the way up Signal Hill when she was caught in the headlights of the rover. She slid to a stop as the truck did the same, and then she heard the single most important voice, "Mom? Mom!"

Alex looked shaky as she hopped out of the vehicle and hurried forward to hug her mother, and with her one good arm, Caralynne hugged back, "Thank God. You're okay?"

"We're all fine. She killed the men who were manning the tower," Alex answered. "She went over the side, but she was wounded. We should send someone out to find her... maybe we should go..."

Her voice clearly revealed her exhaustion, so Caralynne shook her head and squeezed her daughter again, "The marines can handle that. We'll go tell them, but then we're done for the night."

Meeting her mother's eyes, Alex blurted out more information, "Stephanie shot her in the leg, but we think she's alive... so we'll find her another time?"

"Another time," Caralynne confirmed. She then put her hand on her daughter's cheek, "Thank God you're okay."

The warmth of that touch was more calming than

anything else, and Alex closed her eyes to appreciate it. She was still so tense, but she was recovering from the crash, and now her mother was with her.

Then a strange aroma reached her nose.

She stopped, then withdrew her face from her mother's palm and inhaled, "Were you... is that moose smell?"

Caralynne blinked, confused, but decided just to answer obliquely, "Sorry, but you might want to wash your face. I'll explain later. Help me get into the jeep?"

Sitting in the passenger seat with her necktie loose, her collar open, and a faraway stare, Stephanie called out the correction: "It's a Land Rover."

By the time the rover pulled up outside the Caribou Hut, downtown St. John's was alive with soldiers. At least two assault companies had arrived from Fort Waller, and the Royal Newfoundland Constabulary's policemen were in the street as well, helping keep the people of the town out of the way as countless vehicles rolled by.

Regimental Sergeant Major Halloran was heading into the Hut when the new truck arrived, and he paused just long enough to recognize who it was carrying, then to hand off a message to a passing man, "Go get Lord Jimmy, tell him Caralynne and Lady Alex are back."

The soldier hurried off, and Halloran approached the rover as its occupants piled painfully out. Stephanie was stretching her back slightly as she rounded the vehicle, Alex helped her mother over its side, and Strong wheezed as he let his boots touch the tarmac.

"Sergeant Major," he nodded as he recognized the Special Service Regiment's senior soldier, and Halloran shifted his wise eyes between the quartet.

"All in one piece?"

Strong was the first to answer, "I might be in several pieces, but if so they're all caught inside my guts."

Alex grimaced at the mental image those words painted, "Don't think I needed to hear that."

"It was even less funny than the regurgitation joke," Stephanie agreed.

"Who says it's not the truth?" Strong groaned back at them, but before anything more could be said, Jimmy and Annie emerged from the Caribou Hut, a trail of officers behind them.

"You're all alright?" the Viscount's concern was entirely genuine, and it was Caralynne's turn to provide an answer.

"Bumps, bruises, dislocated arms... but breathing."

Jimmy absorbed that report as his eyes scanned the four weary warriors, "She get into the Atlantic?"

Alex nodded this time, "She's wounded, but we think so. We should probably send someone out for a look... there must be a ship waiting for her."

"*Inglefield* has already weighed anchor," Lady Anne stepped up alongside her husband as she spoke. "Todd was awfully mad at all of you for not shooting down Emily when you had the chance."

Of course he was. Alex cast a glance at Stephanie, and saw her friend start to square her shoulders slightly — one of the early signs of defensiveness.

"I'm sure you made the right decision," Jimmy said, preempting any inopportune outbursts from the youngsters. "God knows we need to interrogate her to find out what the hell she's doing. And we'll want you to remember every detail... anything she said, anything she did that hints at where she's been, or where she's gone. But not right now."

Having been through more than his share of battles, Lord Devlin knew better than to try to railroad young warriors into debriefings too quickly — particularly after a night like this one.

"We'll see if *Inglefield* can turn anything up out there," Anne added.

"And I've got Kennedy up with *Skipper Miller*, to see if the radars can do any good."

It was a fairly robust search, but everyone listening knew how difficult it would be. With the advantage of darkness and all sorts of coast nearby where a small boat might shelter, it would be easy for Emily to escape.

But whatever else he was, Todd seemed to be an effective destroyer Captain, and of course the abilities of the skycruisers were peerless in the world... so perhaps they'd turn something up.

Just not likely.

"We'll keep everything under double guard for the foreseeable future," Jimmy decided enough had been said. "For now, you all should patch yourselves up and get some rest. We can debrief tomorrow."

He was being terribly accommodating, and Alex could only nod to acknowledge that, "Really appreciate it."

"Thank you, sir," Stephanie added.

As they both spoke, Jimmy considered the girls in silence. They'd survived one hell of a first test, but there were undoubtedly many lessons to be learned from this night. Work for another day.

"Away with you," the Viscount waved his hand at them. "I'll finish up the search here."

With that he turned away, nodding to the Captains and Majors who'd joined him so they could return to their meeting inside the Hut. Halloran went as well, though Lady Anne remained behind for a moment. Alex and Stephanie both let out long breaths, then moved to lean side-by-side against the rover. Caralynne let her head drop back and then used her good arm to collect her dangling dislocated one, "I need to go see about having this popped back in. Medic which way?"

Anne pointed back through the Hut door, and with a quick nod to her daughter, the Lady headed inside for what was sure to be a pleasant restoration.

That left Strong standing on the sidewalk, and as he unbuttoned his battle dress collar, he started shaking his head, "Well I think I best leave, while I can still manfully pretend that I'm not in huge amounts of pain…"

Lady Anne looked to her misbehaving Sergeant with a stern maternal expression, "I feel obliged to scold you for hurting yourself, but I suppose it was for the greater good. This time."

"Strictly speaking, it was Emily who hurt him," Alex rallied tiredly to the defense of her Colour.

"Threw him through the Bowring store window, in fact," Stephanie added.

Strong frowned — grimaced almost — and glanced at the girls, "Yes, and none of it hurt. But Lady Anne, I can assure you that everything I do is for the greater good."

He overcame his discomfort to grin when he said that, and as the Viscountess rolled her eyes, Alex and Stephanie managed to smile. That took effort, which was why Strong's grin broadened at their approval.

And then, with absolutely perfect timing, a call came from the door of the Caribou Hut.

"Colour!"

A girl who could have been no older than Alex hurried out of the building with a great big smile and her arms wide open. Seeing her approach, Strong braced himself and spread his arms too. When she basically slammed into him for a powerful hug, he couldn't help but wheeze. But other than the obvious discomfort, he seemed to enjoy having a pretty young woman embracing him.

Difficult to fathom why.

Alex, Stephanie and Anne all watched for a whole minute as Strong and Daphne embraced, and then as the girl finally withdrew the Colour turned her slightly to face his charges: "Daphne, this is Lady Alex, and Lieutenant Shylock. I'm working with them now."

Daphne released Strong at that introduction, then turned towards the two girls who were basically propping each other up against the rover.

"How do you do," she nodded... and then she actually curtsied. What was odd about the youthful move was how genuine it appeared — Daphne certainly didn't seem experienced enough to be going with a man twice her age.

Alex tried to make note of that, but she was too tired for it to make much sense. Instead, she answered, "I'd curtsy back, but I'm very awkward."

"She really is," Stephanie reinforced the sentiment. "As evidenced by the fact she didn't even say hello before telling you she's awkward. But we're both pleased to meet you."

They were, though it would have been quite reasonable for someone to think otherwise, given the strange delivery of those greetings. Daphne, however, seemed not to mind.

Turning back to her Sergeant, she made big eyes at him... but again, there was something too innocent about her gaze.

"Colour, would you escort me home to bed?"

With his grin growing, Strong nodded without a hint

of pain, "Always a pleasure."

He cast a quick glance at Anne, who was considering him through narrowed eyes, then back to his officer and his Champion.

"Go on," Stephanie shooed him with a disinterested wave of her hand.

"Don't keep her waiting," Alex added, and with that permission the Colour held out his arm so Daphne could take it, then set off down the street with a walk that looked rather jaunty.

That was quite a show, and both Alex and Stephanie watched it with as much interest as they could manage in their exhausted states. Which wasn't much.

But it was still enough for them to detect some of the b'ys of 'C' Company noticing the Colour and his pretty young girl, and grinning at each other. Damn that Mike Strong, what *would* he do?

Somehow Alex suspected it wasn't what those men expected, but she was very tired, and decided not to comment because she was probably wrong.

Stephanie, however, was less discreet: "Is it just me, or is that girl not nearly worldly enough to actually be *going* with our dear Sergeant?"

Alex perked up very slightly at that, then nodded, "I know, right?"

Both girls then turned their gazes to Lady Anne, who simply had to know everything that happened in the Special

Service Regiment. The Viscountess was watching Strong's departure, but feeling gazes landing on her, she glanced back towards the girls.

"That's not for me to say," was her answer, and Alex frowned earnestly.

"But I was just held at gunpoint," she pouted.

"And I was thrown into the air, and then caught, and then she landed on me," Stephanie sounded equally forlorn. "She's not as light as she looks."

"I have been eating more," Alex added. "So that must have hurt."

Lady Anne just stared at them both, then smiled and shook her head.

"Guilt trip not working?" Stephanie confirmed.

"It's for him to tell you," the Viscountess answered. "You two are good for him, though. Believe me when I tell you that."

Somehow both the young Champion and her officer did believe that, but they had no more time to try to pry additional information from Lady Anne. Caralynne emerged from the Hut, her arm restored and her expression masking the pain for the sake of her girls, "That was pleasant. So, home and bed time?"

She doubted either Stephanie or Alex would get much sleep on this particular night, but it would be worth making the attempt.

Taking a deep breath, it was the young Champion who

answered first: "I really want a bath."

"She smells like moose," her Lieutenant said.

"Better than smelling like gull," was Alex's counter.

Then both girls started to laugh... and kept laughing. They were so exhausted, and still getting to grips with the risks they'd taken that night. Fortunately, they could call on terrible jokes to diffuse the tension, at least for a little while.

Stepping towards the rover, Caralynne made a mental note to ask what her daughter's moose thing was about.

Then she stopped.

It was Lady Anne who identified the problem for them all: "Do any of you know how to drive that thing?"

Of course none of them knew how to drive a rover — two Champions and an accomplished horsewoman had no business behind the wheel.

"What would Mike Strong do?" Caralynne muttered that question to herself with a shake of her head. But it was fine; after a brief round of grumbling, the trio secured a corporal from one of the assault companies to take them home. Their night was over.

As the Land Rover carrying Alex, Stephanie and Caralynne pulled away from the Caribou Hut, it passed two men who were watching the events of the night with great interest. Both were wearing gray trench coats — which no one but them actually called *trench* coats — and both bore studied expressions that suggested they were not pleased with what they were seeing.

"How many dead is that... six tonight, besides the ones at the Fort?" the slightly taller one asked, and the shorter one shook his head.

"I thought it was seven, here. Two at Cabot Tower. Plus thirty-four in New York."

Taking a deep breath, the taller graycoat shook his head, "I'm not going to say what I'm thinking. But you know I'm thinking it."

"We both are."

For a few more minutes they stood silent, watching as assault companies from the Special Service Regiment moved up and down the street and RNC Constables kept the crowds of onlookers at bay. Despite the danger of Emily possibly making a return, everyone wanted to see the commotion... wanted to know what torment had wrecked their town.

But the two graycoats could only stomach so much of it. Turning away, they fell into step, first heading up Water Street, then turning up the long hill that led away from the harbor towards the Basilica. As they went, the shorter one sighed, "I know the whole 'greater good' thing actually means something this time... but..."

He trailed off as he forced himself not to voice his complete distaste, but because they'd been together through war and peace, the taller man knew precisely what his friend meant, "She would have done the same thing if we weren't here... it would just have been worse. And this is the only way to save the world."

The shorter one winced, "Save the *world*?"

"Admittedly that sounded corny, but yeah," the taller one confirmed.

And he was right. But no one else knew, and wouldn't for a long time. For now both men just had to have faith that their plans, and the plans of their unusual sponsors, would in fact prevent the disaster that was on the horizon. Dwelling on that fact would do no good... they had to keep moving forward, and keep restraining Emily's temper.

Because after a night like this, they could only imagine how nasty she could really get...

"They don't have raccoons here, right?"

The taller one blinked at his shorter friend's unexpected question, "Um, no. Seriously?"

"It's dark, and we're here without our usual safety net. That makes them more dangerous."

The taller graycoat shook his head, "You could kill any of them with a—"

"Don't finish the sentence," the shorter one interrupted, and the taller one did as he was told.

Things were altogether too strange for these two, but they had to hold to their belief that, in working with Emily, they'd ultimately stop a grave disaster.

It would be a long few years...

EPILOGUE

There really was no chance of either Alex or Stephanie sleeping. As the midnight hour passed, both girls took their turns in the bathtub, painfully washing away some of the evidence of the drubbing they'd received.

The more dirt they cleaned off, and the more bruises they discovered, the more reality started to settle in. They'd truly been in a life and death fight that night... a hell of a way to start their adventures as Champion and Lieutenant.

When they'd emerged from their baths, both girls did what was most natural on nights when they couldn't sleep: they retreated to the kitchen. In winter, that room tended to be the warmest one in the house, and though the temperate August made temperature irrelevant, it was still the focal point of the Smith home.

Usually, though, the mood wasn't quite so somber.

Sitting at the table as they both nursed cups of warm milk, Alex and Stephanie found themselves unable to banter with each other. Both were caught up remembering, and realizing the scale of the risks they'd taken.

Chasing Emily had been reckless, and Alex probably shouldn't have done it. If the savage-born woman hadn't stopped herself, it was quite possible the newest Champion would be dead. And what if that magazine safety hadn't worked? What would being shot have felt like?

While those questions haunted her friend, Stephanie was tormented by the fact that she could have stopped Emily cold. One shot... she'd had the rogue in her sights on Water Street — could have actually shot her like Todd had said. Shooting the gun from her hands instead? What foolishness was that? Even her godfather would have objected — gunfighters didn't showboat during a fight. At least not the ones who meant to survive.

Such were the questions that circled both friends after midnight. As darkness pressed in through the kitchen window and crowded the table, their mutual self-scolding thoughts were a clear reflection of the high expectations they held for themselves.

And standing in the kitchen door, Smith watched with some consternation. It was unusual for the former-drifter to be ill-at-ease, but the fact that Emily had come back, had fought his girls and had killed more people... and that he'd been stuck in his house the whole time... the possibilities were tormenting him too. He and Caralynne would speak of everything that had happened once she was out of the bath, but for now even the American's calm was shaken.

Watching his girls grapple with the 'what-ifs' wasn't helping... but that was something he could fix.

Moving quietly into the kitchen, Smith leaned against

the counter in front of the window, purposely blocking out the dark night. Neither girl seemed to notice his arrival, but that was alright — he just started talking, saying what he figured was best.

"Wondering 'what if' is important," the former-drifter said. "That's how you learn."

Blinking a couple of times, Alex looked to her father, and then Stephanie considered him with a frown.

"Thing is, whatever could have happened, didn't. You both looked after each other, as was right, and you came back home. Some other people didn't get to do that. You can be sad over them dying, and scared for what might have happened... but be happy that you're back here. Because I sure am."

Smith didn't consider himself to be a good man with words, but he was a great one for being direct about his thoughts and feelings. No speech could fully relieve these two of their dark contemplations... but somehow, daylight did start to appear in the dark kitchen.

And then Smith finished off with the most important thing: "I'm proud of both of you."

That was the absolute truth, and after he said it the girls seemed ready to digest his dialogue. He decided to let them do that in peace, so he moved away from the counter and advanced towards the kitchen table. There Stephanie looked up at him with a soft smile, "Thanks Uncle Smith."

She reached up with her free hand, and he squeezed

it with a nod. Alex was standing up halfway by the time her father turned to her, and she hugged him, letting out a long breath as she did. Some of her tension began to uncoil, and then Smith kissed his daughter on the forehead before leaving the room.

Sitting back down, Alex found herself staring into her cup of milk. It was white, just like her coat had been... and would be again, provided the cleaners were some sort of magical wizards with the power to obliterate dirt.

That thought made her frown, and looking across the table, Stephanie correctly predicted her preoccupation, "I'm sure it'll clean up fine. And if it could survive today, it's going to last for quite a while."

"I suppose," Alex conceded, then looked up at her friend. "I probably should have picked green, though."

Stephanie half-shrugged, then took a sip of her milk before answering, "It would have matched my nail polish."

"I still don't believe you have that."

"Oh I do," the American girl answered. "You might have to show me how to put it on, though. I led a sheltered childhood."

That was obviously the truth, so Alex agreed, "Yes. The gunplay and horse riding has left you a complete social wreck. You're almost as awkward as me."

"I would have *shot* gull Casanova," Stephanie offered.

"I would have tried, but missed," Alex replied.

Those words reflected a little too much genuine doubt,

and noticing a frown beginning to crease her friend's face again, Stephanie leaned across the table and covered Alex's free hand with her own, "Hey. You wear the coat well."

Looking up, Alex stared at her friend for a moment. However dangerous recent events had been, her father was right: they had taken care of each other... and they were very lucky to have the chance to do this together. Whatever came next, it would be the pair of them — and Strong — who met it head-on.

She just had to figure out a way to keep her coat clean.

Very gradually, the thought of everything to come brought a smile to Alex's lips. As her mood brightened, she turned her free hand over so it could grasp her friend's, and she rallied: "I do look reasonably amazing when I'm wearing it. Maybe even irresistible."

Stephanie matched her friend's smile, "Let's not get carried away. Though I'm sure the gull is going to be kicking himself."

Of course he would, because aside from becoming the victim of stress-relieving jokes, the Casanova entirely missed out.

"I know!" Alex's smile broadened. "If he'd just played his cards right... he could have had himself a whitecoat."

Well, that was probably pushing it.

JOIN ALEX, STEPHANIE AND STRONG FOR THEIR NEXT MISSION:

THE CHAMPIONS OF 1941 PART 1

FIREBOX

KENNETH TAM

EBOOK RELEASE: JANUARY 2013

PRINT RELEASE (AS PART OF 1941 OMNIBUS): NOVEMBER 2013

FOR THE LATEST: CHAMPIONSOF1940.COM

ALSO AVAILABLE FROM ICEBERG PUBLISHING

DEFENSE COMMAND
BY KENNETH TAM

If you enjoyed meeting Lady Alex Smith and Lieutenant Stephanie Shylock, you seriously need to meet **Captain Karen McMaster** in:

1. The Rogue Commodore (June 2006) | ebook
2. The Almost Coup (June 2006) | ebook
3. The Hawke Mission (Nov. 2006) | ebook
4. The Independent Squadron (Nov. 2006) | ebook
Omnibus 1. 2231: Mars Against Empire (Jan. 2010) | Print Book

5. The Gallant Few (June 2007) | ebook
6. The Jupiter Patrol (June 2007) | ebook
7. The Sinope Affair (December 2007) | ebook
8. The Dark Cruise (December 2007) | ebook
Omnibus 2. 2232: Chase Into Blackness (Jan. 2010) | Print Book

9. The Canary Wars (July 2008) | ebook
10. The Forge Fires (July 2008) | ebook
11. The Mercury Assault (July 2009) | ebook
12. The Fleet Clash (July 2009) | ebook
Omnibus 3. 2233: Reap The Whirlwind (Jan. 2010) | Print Book

13. The Mars Convention (July 2010) | ebook
14. The Egesta Crisis (July 2010) | ebook
15. The Pax Terra (July 2011) | ebook
16. The Articles Of Empire (July 2011) | ebook
Omnibus 4. 2234: Victory From Peace (July 2012) | Print Book

17. Tapestries Of Blood (July 2012) | ebook
18. Memories Of Angels (July 2012) | ebook
19. Acts Of War (July 2012) | ebook
20. Enemies Of Empire (July 2012) | ebook
Omnibus 5. 2235: The World Is Broken (July 2012) | Print Book

WWW.DEFENSECOMMAND.NET

ALSO AVAILABLE FROM ICEBERG PUBLISHING

HIS MAJESTY'S
NEW WORLD
by KENNETH TAM

Can't wait for the next mission with Alex, Stephanie and
Strong? Use the break to catch up on the adventures
shared by Caralynne, Smith, Jimmy, Annie and the b'ys of
the Royal Newfoundland Regiment on the new world.

The *His Majesty's New World* novels by Kenneth Tam
Book One: The Grasslands (April 2008)
Book Two: The Frontier (April 2009)
Book Three: The Reprisal (June 2010)
Book Four: The Expedition (July 2011)
Book Five: The Badlands (July 2012)
Book Six: The Empire (July 2012)

The complete series is now available in both print and
ebook formats. For more information, visit:

www.newworldempire.com

ALSO AVAILABLE FROM ICEBERG PUBLISHING

KENNETH TAM'S
EQUATIONS NOVELS

The Earthers evolved after humans were driven from the Earth by an intelligent bio-weapon dubbed 'Omega'. They are faster, stronger, smarter, wiser, *better* than humans, and they are the only hope for the survivors of the human race as an interstellar war between two great alien powers absorbs the galaxy. But all is not as it seems, and the humans and the Earthers face challenges that overshadow the wars of alien empires and threaten to destroy their civilizations...

The Equations Novels by Kenneth Tam
Book One: The Human Equation (Oct 2003)
Book Two: The Alien Equation (May 2004)
Book Three: The Renegade Equation (Dec 2004)
Book Four: The Earther Equation (July 2005)
Book Five: The Genesis Equation (July 2006)
Book Six: The Vengeance Equation (July 2007)
Book Seven: The Nemesis Equation (July 2008)
Book Eight: The Destiny Equation (July 2009)

The complete series is now available in both print and ebook formats. For more information, visit:

www.earther.net

ABOUT THE AUTHOR

Born in 1984 in St. John's, Newfoundland, Kenneth Tam is the author of more than thirty novels of science fiction and alternate history. He is also a Partner in Iceberg Publishing, a company he founded with his parents in 2002. Since the release of his first novel in 2003, he has traveled extensively across Canada, and has appeared as a guest author at numerous science fiction events.

Outside his writing, Kenneth holds both a BA and an MA in military history. For one year in 2006-2007, he was a Balsillie Fellow at the Centre for International Governance Innovation, where he worked for former UN Ambassador Paul Heinbecker. He subsequently spent two years on staff for Canadian Member of Parliament Peter Braid, serving as a Communications Consultant. He is presently an advisor with Sun Life Financial in Waterloo, Ontario.

You can follow Kenneth on Twitter (@KTam_Iceberg), though he's not very adept at tweeting... yet.

www.ingramcontent.com/pod-product-compliance
Lightning Source LLC
Chambersburg PA
CBHW021223250626
47155CB00008B/2913